MW00931141

# Blissful Encounters

## By

## Dimitria DesJardins

Published by Wagner Wolf LLC

www.facebook.com/dimitria.desjardins

WagnerWolfPublishing@yahoo.com

www.WagnerWolf.com

# Blissful Encounters

## Dimitria DesJardins

*For the women, men, and couples who dare to experience a unique adventure, this book is for you!*

# Table of Contents

## INTRODUCTION

Mia here. So I'm a single woman. I supported my boyfriend as he realized all of his career dreams. I postponed most of my career dreams in hopes of having children and being a stay-at-home mom someday, which, of course, never happened. After years of betrayal, frustration, and sexual disappointment, I found out that this joker was cheating on me across the country! I left his ass, but that was not easy for me. I always put our relationship and home first. Now this is the first time that I'm putting myself before Ken and his stupid needs. I'm devastated by the decision, but deep down; I know it was only a matter of time.

So I've saved a lot of money over the years, and I decided to kick things into high gear. I'm going to travel abroad– something I have yet to do, despite traveling all around the U.S. I'm gonna go to beautiful Europe and use my foreign language skills for once. I'm going to visit some of the most romantic places, meet some really cool people, and have the most explosive sex of my life. Hey – a girl can dream!

I wrote all about my trip in my journal, and now I'm letting you read it! Follow me through some old, historic cities and new, unforgettable adventures.  Journey with me as I rediscover myself and pursue the things that are important to me. Try to keep up with me during my hot European summer. See if you can handle my Blissful Encounters!

# "Early On"

## 30 April, 2013

I met my boyfriend Ken six years ago at a nightclub. At the time, I was single and enjoying life as an immigration attorney here in New Orleans. I was content. I had a beautiful apartment, traveled quite a bit, and spent time with my friends every chance that I got. I wasn't particularly interested in meeting anyone new, so I was not looking to date. One Saturday night while out on the town with my friends, I saw this man having a drink at a small table with his friend in a nightclub. I was fascinated with his looks. Ken is a very handsome, tall, man with a deep dark complexion. He has an impressive muscular build and has very sharp, distinct facial features. His small, sharp nose, narrow jaw line, thin lips, and chocolate eyes are a constant reminder of his French/Creole background.

He looked confident to me and that was a huge turn on. He caught me looking at him and I guess he figured out that I found him to be intriguing. It was not long before he made his way over to me and asked me to dance. It was very romantic. We spent the evening together dancing, having drinks, and chatting. We exchanged numbers and began to date. After a few months, we developed a relationship and began to care about each other deeply. The sex was good enough; I was just so into him that sex was not a top priority for me. He was okay with foreplay. It did not bother me at the time that I had never had an orgasm with him. I assumed that would come in time. Little did I know that my ultimate pleasure would be my responsibility! He loved it when I went down on him. He always climaxed. I never disappointed him. I did think every now and again, "Why won't he do that for me?" I didn't worry about it, but that was a sign that his pleasure was more important than mine. It was a disappointment, but not enough for me to stop dating him. I figured that if I left him, it would be selfish and irrational. After all, who would break up with someone who could not satisfy them sexually? That would be ridiculous, or so I thought.

I never made too much of Kenny being distant. He was not the warm-and-fuzzy type of man and I just accepted him as he was. I always thought that he loved me. I thought he expressed his love for me by surprising me with trips to Vegas and Miami or tickets to concerts. We never really had conversations per se. He would talk about his workday and I would talk about mine, but it was all small talk. He did not seem comfortable talking about really deep issues. I began to wonder if he had someone else who he really talked about his concerns at work, his goals and his frustrations with. I always shared my thoughts with Ken. No matter what he shared or did not share with me, I always made sure that I kept the lines of communication open on my end.

After several years of living together, we stopped kissing. I took notice and I did mention it to him, but he gave me some lame excuse that it was not a big deal. When a couple stops kissing passionately, there is trouble brewing. Kissing is so intimate and special. It is one of the most pleasurable and exciting expressions of attraction or love in a relationship with someone. We lost that. Ken did not even miss it. I did though. But like everything else, I dealt with it and just suppressed my feelings about it.

Month after month, I was hoping to become pregnant. I took my temperature and made copious notes on my calendar about when I was fertile and which were the best days to have sex. Despite my diligent efforts, I never became pregnant. It never occurred to me that perhaps it was not meant to be. Ken was so aloof about it - I sometimes wondered if he had a vasectomy and just never told me. Knowing what I know now, I wouldn't put it past the scumbag.

With his job as a sales representative, he did a lot of traveling. He always told me where he was going, but I never got details or itineraries from him – no hotel names or addresses. I never questioned his whereabouts because I trusted him. However, when I traveled with my friends overnight, he had to have all the information and would even call the hotel to verify that I was staying there! This guy was unbelievable! He was doing God knows what when he was traveling, but I would just hang out with my girlfriends. I was always loyal to him no matter what he suspected.

One time when he returned home from a trip, he smelled like perfume. I asked him about it and he just said his client gave him a hug. I didn't make a big deal about it. But later, I checked his pants' pockets and found a dinner receipt. It was a large bill. I assumed he took some floozy out to dinner. They ordered lots of wine and fancy drinks. I thought it was way too much alcohol consumption for a client. Again, I tried not to make too much of it, but I took note of everything. The final straw came when I found bright pink lipstick on his shirt that had recently been dry-cleaned. The lipstick was not on the collar but near the bottom of his shirt – the area where the shirt would be tucked in! I confronted him about that too and he just made it seem like I was paranoid. I pretty much knew at that moment that he was cheating, but I could not bring myself to really do anything about it. It would be a long time before I actually got the nerve to do something about my suspicions. I loved this man very much for whatever reason. Plus, in the back of mind, I thought that no one would really want me because of my age. Most men want younger women. I am no longer in the "younger" category. As the months passed by, I slowly gained the strength to be less trusting and more reasonable about the person I was spending my life with.

I knew that when I finally decided to make a move, it would be a big one!

# "Second Thoughts"

## 20 May, 2013

So many times I thought about leaving. I planned it. I fantasized about it. But when there was a window of opportunity, I couldn't do it. I kept hoping to become pregnant, thinking that it would save my relationship. The baby that I had planned for, hoped for, and dreamed about never became a reality. My life had purpose with the prospect of becoming a mom. The older I became, the stronger my urge was to get pregnant. I wanted to experience the feeling of a bird fluttering in my stomach that I heard so many women talk about. I wondered if I would suffer from morning sickness or have cravings. Getting pregnant became an obsession because I knew time was running out for me to be able to conceive.

In order to maximize my chances of getting pregnant, I worked out avidly, ate right and took excellent care of myself. Despite my obsession with maternity clothes, creating a nursery and watching baby birthing shows, my lover was nowhere near as enthusiastic as I was. He was more concerned with my curves morphing into 'sloppy' fat. He made no bones about how he felt about overweight women. He was repulsed by them. He never appreciated the beauty in bigger women who could not focus on their bodies and keep them '22-year-old-tight', as I called it. I became obsessed with looking presentable at least. Therefore, I always tried to look halfway decent. I didn't want to lose Kenny's attention or do anything that would make him look elsewhere. Although I was never thin, he rarely complained. He did make snide comments here and there. He was sure to let me know when I gained a little too much after the holidays or after we returned from vacations. I felt like I was on eggshells with what I put in my mouth and going to the gym. Meanwhile, his belly slowly got bigger and bigger, which really annoyed me.

Ken was also very content with our life as a successful couple sans children. We traveled quite a bit domestically. There were many cities around the country that we knew like the back of our hands. We had a beautiful home, luxurious cars, and impressive properties.

I had all the jewelry a woman could ask for. With all of the amenities though, I was so unhappy and unfulfilled. When we made love, I felt empty. He rarely satisfied me. It was as if he was always distracted – his mind was elsewhere. I never had an orgasm with him, but sex was still good at times. He was not interested in making sure I felt pleasure. Everything was mechanical with us. He would very rarely go down on me, but when he did, it was not for very long and certainly not long enough to make me have an orgasm. I did not feel comfortable telling him what turned me on. I was not even sure about what did turn me on. I just wanted to become pregnant and the only way for that to happen was through sex. In my mind, I did not have to enjoy it. I just had to be present when at least one of us was in the mood or when I was ovulating.

I tried to talk to Ken about my feelings but he was very dismissive. He felt that I should be satisfied with all of the material things that I had. He did not understand that I needed to feel loved, respected and needed as a woman, not as an object. With my frustrations growing, I felt myself becoming vulnerable. I started to notice men at the gym, at the market, and at the mall. I began to watch porn. I watched women enjoy sex and express themselves so passionately. I became jealous of them at first, but then, I started to admire them. I admired their confidence and how well they knew their bodies.

I had to get to know my body myself with or without Ken's help. I decided one night to pleasure myself while Ken was away on business. After taking a warm bubble bath, I poured myself a glass of wine and watched some porn. It was a movie with a man fucking the shit out of his girlfriend. First, he ate her pussy voraciously. I noticed how he methodically focused on her clit. He sucked on it perfectly and steadily. Her legs were draped over his back while her hands tenderly caressed his ears, guiding his tongue deeper into her wet spot. He was ever so patient. It took her a while but he was determined to make her feel ecstasy. His patience paid off. After slowly licking and sucking on her clit like a pro, she let out a deep, loud moan while she arched her back. Her lover was so pleased. Just as she finished, he rammed his large, hard dick inside of her. She yelled in delight as he pumped her pussy with intense, long strokes. It didn't take long for him to let out a moan and squirt his warm, delicious treat into her silkiness. He was thrilled that he made his lover climax so hard. He felt strong and powerful. I wanted to feel like her. After viewing such a hot video, I was totally turned on. My juices were flowing; I was relaxed and ready to get to know myself better. I laid on my stomach and slightly spread my legs. I started to play with my clit. I was so wet and slippery that my fingers slid off it quickly. I put my two fingers back into position - I was determined to do this. I started to think back to the video. I pretended to be the woman in the video. I want to feel a man between my legs eating me so tenderly and perfectly. I feel my heartbeat pumping stronger and stronger. My pussy is getting hot and even wetter. Way off in the distance, I feel this warm sensation of ecstasy approaching. I have never felt this before. I start to moan. This sensation becomes stronger and stronger. It is somewhat overwhelming, but in a good way. All of a sudden, I let out a moan. Slow, strong waves of electricity emanate through my body. I feel so warm and overcome with sexual pleasure. This is what I've been missing! I want to feel like this all of the time!

Why couldn't Ken do this to me or make me feel this way?

I resent that I had to make this happen myself instead of him wanting to take the time to please me. A door has been opened now. I refuse to go back to "darkness" and not experience true pleasure. I think things may start to change now. Shit – they need to!

# "Enlightenment Phase"

## 23 May, 2013

When Ken returns from his trip, I am determined to get him into bed to see if we can make some magic. I pick him up from the airport and we go out to dinner. We have a great time. We get back home. I put on some Marvin Gaye and he makes us some strong drinks. Everything is perfect.

We embrace and then kiss. I feel him getting aroused and I get excited. Again, I pretend to be the woman in the porno. I want to be her. I want to feel that feeling I experienced the night before. Soon, we are naked on the living room floor. I am surprised by this because Ken is a 'bedroom-missionary-position' kind of guy. He lays on top of me; I am already wet and ready for an unbelievable performance of sorts. He begins to pump me. There is no kissing, no emotion. I try to reach for his lips but he turns his head. I wonder if he is thinking about someone else, wishing she were here with him instead of me.

I can tell he is about to cum. I quickly wrap my legs around his back hoping that will help this along for me before he finishes. No luck. He cums moments later and I am absolutely deflated. He won't go down on me now because he came inside me and doesn't like tasting his own cum. I get up and get halfway dressed. I am not only disappointed, but angry. How dare he not want to please me after six years of being with me? I have been nothing but a faithful, loving partner.

After this disappointing and frustrating session, I begin to contemplate the possibility of an exit. It was scary but I thought it was time. He would be leaving once again on a business trip. I planned to make a surprise visit to him this time. He was going to San Francisco – a place he went rather often. I long suspected that he had some hoochie out there. I found myself putting things together. Ken had his own bank account that I had no access to. He smelled like perfume at times. He's had lipstick on his cheeks and collars before. And he couldn't always get it up for no good reason when everything else was perfect.

It's almost as if his dick already had enough action and it couldn't perform anymore. After all, Ken isn't some strong, virile 20-year-old.

Everything was starting to become more and more suspicious to me. He was hiding something. I could feel it. If he was indeed cheating, I would need hard evidence before ending it.

The time for his week-long stay in California was approaching. Like always, he gave me dates but never specific itineraries, which I always found to be odd. Before he leaves, I ask him for the hotel name and address. He refuses. I ask him why he never wants to divulge that information and he just replies, "Why do you care all of a sudden?" I said, "I was just curious. No big deal. But I know for sure that you would not go for that shit if it were me traveling!" Even though I plan to sneak out to San Fran, I need to know where I am going. I buy the ticket and wait. Two days before he leaves, luck is on my side! A confirmation email was sent to our common email address. I opened it, downloaded it, then deleted it. I pretended that I would be busy with my girlfriends during his stay. I take him to the airport and pretend to drive home. Instead, I park at the next terminal and catch the next flight out. I am elated that the weather is perfect and his flight departs on time. My flight also leaves on time, and I arrive in San Francisco about six hours after he does. I am very nervous. Am I doing the right thing? What if he is by himself? Then I would look dumb as hell.

I was willing to take the chance. My gut tells me that he is with someone and I am determined to follow that feeling. I promise myself that I will follow to my intuition more.

My reservation is at a nearby hotel. I call the hotel to make sure he's checked in. I tell the front desk that I am his wife and I ask what room he's in. They don't give me the information over the phone; I have to go there in person. Once I arrive, my heart is beating out of my chest. I approach the front desk and tell them, "Hello. I'm Mrs. Ken Devereux. I can't reach my husband. His cell phone is dead and he needs to know that I made it to San Francisco." The receptionist asks me for identification. I show him my license. He then calls Ken's room, but lucky for me, there's no answer and there's a long line behind me. The receptionist smiles and gives me the key and the room number. He is anxious to help the other guests. Once I have the key in my hand, I feel a sense of power and also helplessness at the same time. I know what I will probably see in that room - he will be making passionate love to a little tramp.

The room number is 316. I locate the elevator and take it to the third floor. I feel a panic attack coming on but I calm myself down. I have not even reached the room yet. I have to regain my composure. Somehow, somewhere, I find it. I look for the signs that direct me to room 316. I make a right, find the room and just as I suspect, I hear noises – lovemaking noises. I am mad as hell! I regain my calmness as I open the door. I insert the key and am not prepared for what I see. Silly me. I thought I would see Ken on top of a woman pumping her in the missionary position. That was not what I saw at all.

Once I open the door, the room is brightly lit. I see this beautiful, busty woman sitting on Ken's face. She was fucking his face with her pussy. Ken was in awe as her wet pussy humped his tongue. She was in total ecstasy. They did not even know that I opened the door and was watching them for what seemed like minutes. I eventually yelled, "Kenny?" She jumped off his face and he sat up. Her juices were dripping all over. It was disgusting to me. Not because of what was on his face but that he hardly ever did that to me. I felt betrayed, very angry, and hurt. I screamed, "How could you do that with her and not with me? I'm your woman, you asshole!!" I had my ammunition. I got what I came for. And boy did I get it! I could not breathe. I was heartbroken. My whole world was shattered. Even though my relationship was not the best, it was mine and he messed it up. I had to pick up the pieces. I was in a daze. I ran out of the room, down the hall and into the elevator. I left out through the lobby and caught the first cab that I saw. Soon, I heard my phone going off. It was him. I had no interest in speaking to him. He starts to blow up my phone. He knows he has screwed up but he doesn't think that I will leave him. He just thinks he will be in the dog house for a minute. It will cost him but the price will be much more than he could have imagined. He embarrassed me and snatched my dream of having a baby. He will pay for this. I will see to it.

I pull myself together and go to the airport. I changed my flight so that I could leave right away. It cost me $500 to change my ticket, but it was worth every penny. I decide never to return to San Francisco again, even though it is one of my favorite cities. On my flight, my life flashes before my eyes. What will I tell our friends and family? I then realize, he screwed up so he will have to explain everything because I did nothing wrong.

When I get home, I am mentally and physically exhausted. Ken is still blowing up my phone. He called me 18 times since I left San Francisco. He is panicking. Good! I gather up all his shit and put everything in garbage bags because that's what he is to me – garbage! I put it all out on the porch. I change the locks the next morning and I will soon get one of the best lawyers in New Orleans.

## "The End Is Near"

## 24 May, 2013

Ken made it back from his trip and he was frantic. I was distraught, exhausted, and disappointed. I had no energy to fight for what we had. All of our property was in both of our names. What a mess! The way I was feeling, he could have it all, but I know that I would regret that decision later. I just ask him to leave and to take his things. He refuses at first. I already changed the locks so he was not getting back in. Luckily, he appeases me and agrees to leave. I am relieved but so sad. The realization of having to start my life over without him is daunting. But, I have no choice. Tonight, I will have brownie sundae, take a sleeping pill and then have the most awesome sleep ever.

# "Wrapping Things Up"

## 9 June, 2013

I speak with my lawyer and because we never married and had no kids, the split is pretty cut and dry. I made sure that my name was on everything. Even though I was not very smart in recognizing Kenny's antics over the years, I am smart about our investments. Not only did I partly own a fair amount of real estate with him, we both owned numerous stocks, some gold, and had substantial savings. I was saving to stay home and not have to work for at least five or ten years to take care of our kids. I was living comfortably. Now I have to decide what to do with all of the money that I've saved. I am thinking about going to Europe. I have a passport; I update it every ten years just in case. Now is the time to use it. Summer is supposed to be a great time to go. It will be crowded, but a fun time. I decided to plan my trip for a few weeks in July. Summer in Europe sounds wonderful. I can't wait!

# "In Flight"

## 18 July, 2013

As I wait in the airport, I am anxious about my new life without Ken. I am very scared but I am content with my decision. I am not thinking about meeting anyone new. I just want to get away, far away from him, and everything that reminds me of him.

I am feeling relaxed, wearing my jeans skirt, t-shirt and sneakers. I barely have any makeup on. For once, I am not all dolled up. I look plain and simple. I really don't have the energy to be girly today.

They begin boarding. I eagerly get in line in hopes of being able to stow my luggage above my actual seat. As I walk further and further back, I finally find my seat. It's in the rear of the plane, which is perfect. I am not in the mood to be around people. The last row is private and the restroom is right there. This eight-hour flight is looking pretty good. The weather is cooperating. We are leaving on time and the flight is not all the way full. As I pull out my book to read and get ready to pop my sleeping pill, I notice this very handsome young man board the plane. He is sharp! He is tall, handsome, and well-dressed. He is a black guy and I even notice his bright smile as he displays his pearly whites at a flight attendant. I like a man who's well groomed. When people care about their outward appearance, it speaks volumes about their character. I am very picky about who I date, so I notice the little things!

This handsome man continues to walk further and further back onto the plane. I think to myself, 'Could his seat be next to mine?' As I look on either side of me, there are two empty seats. He continues to head in my direction. I am getting very nervous at this point. I didn't want to be bothered with people, but he is different! Just my luck, he sits down to my left. I am stunned! 'Is my luck changing?' I think to myself. From his looks and manly smell, things are indeed changing for the better. As he places his luggage overhead, I check out his body all the while I take in the aroma of his strong, masculine cologne. It is turning me on, which I hate to admit. He is also very fit; it is obvious that he works out. Check! He has a great smile and lovely hands. Check! Not only are his hands well-groomed, but they are very large. I let my imagination wander as I fantasize that his hands are proportionate to his penis size. I bet it is big. He is tall with big hands. How could he not have a big dick? I then feel a small grin spread across my face. I take notice at his exotic features. His skin is a warm chocolate, reddish color. His hair is jet black and curly but cut close. Despite his darker complexion, his mesmerizing hazel eyes pop out and seem to put me in a trance whenever he glances at me. I feel my heart racing and a constant grin develop on my face. He reminds me of the actor, Giancarlo Esposito, but his hazel eyes are everything! As he notices me observe him intriguingly, he smiles at me and says, "Hello. How are you?" I respond, "Fine, thank you and yourself?" He says, "I'm good." He then asks me, "Is this your first trip to Paris?" I tell him yes it is. He says, "You will absolutely love it. I come every two years. The scenery, the food, the shopping and the ambiance are simply electrifying. You will see." He has me sold. I hang on to his every word. Within a few short minutes, this fine stranger has my full attention. I love this eye candy that is before me. I hope he finds me attractive too. I see him surreptitiously checking out my body. Even though I am not dressed to impress, my simple, plain clothes have caught his attention. He can see that I have intriguing curves.

It's time for us to buckle up and taxi down the runway while the flight attendants go over the rules and regulations. I try to pay attention, but it is difficult. He asks me my name and I tell him, "Mia". He says, "Oh, Italian for mine". I said, "Yes. How did you know that? Do you speak Italian?" He says, "Yes, I speak French and Italian. My dad is half Italian. My grandmother only spoke Italian with me when I was small. I kept it up and then took French in school and did a study abroad in college." I say, "That is very interesting because I am a polyglot. I speak Spanish, French, Italian, Portuguese, and Greek. I have friends from different backgrounds and I practice my languages with them. I ask him, "What's your name?" He tells me, "Jack. It is really Giacomo but I go by Jack. Giacomo is too complicated for most people to pronounce. My family calls me that or, when I travel to Italy, I go by Giacomo. Other than that, I like Jack."

"Pleasure to meet you, Jack," I reply. "Likewise", he says.

I begin to yawn. Jack disappointingly says, "Don't fall asleep on me. I was looking forward to talking with you for a while." I wish I had not taken that damn sleeping pill. I had just taken it before I saw his fine-ass get on the plane. I am so mad at myself. Now, I have to fight to stay awake. When the flight attendants come around, I request a soda. That should wake me up. I want to chat with him for at least a little while. I want to hear more about this guy.

We take off. I have always enjoyed taking off. I am excited to know that I will be in Europe in a few hours. I ask myself, 'Why did I wait so long to travel overseas?' I feel like I wasted too much time with that idiot, Ken. I missed out on doing a lot of things. I could have climbed the corporate ladder more than I did, but I was planning for that baby to come anytime. I have to put that behind me and just look forward to my future without him. I am actually starting to embrace my new life. Jack definitely is right-on-time. The first leg of this trip should be pretty interesting to say the least.

After a few hours, we've eaten, laughed, talked, and joked. It's time to go to sleep. We have our blankets and all of the lights in the cabin go out except for those few annoying passengers who insist on reading at 11pm when everyone else wants to sleep. I hate that! Nonetheless, Jack and I have the back row to ourselves, which is kind of interesting. I feel myself leaning on his shoulder. The sleeping pill has kicked in. He doesn't seem to mind. It feels comforting just being close to another man who doesn't seem to be an asshole. I like it.

Not long after I doze off, Jack falls asleep upon my head. We sleep for a few hours that way. After a while, I wake up. I have to go to the bathroom. Luckily, there is a washroom in the back of the plane, and there are several others up front. With the plane half full, hardly anyone comes all the way to the back. The privacy comes as unusual luck. I really have to go. It's difficult using airplane toilets; there is very little room to move around.

Unbeknownst to me, Jack wakes up and discovers that I have disappeared. I guess he assumes that I went to the bathroom. Apparently, he has the wicked idea to pay me a visit in the loo. With the plane dark and everyone asleep, he anxiously walks to the back of the plane and sees the restroom is occupied. He knocks to make sure it is me. I am just finishing up as I hear a noise at the door. I am baffled that someone would knock on this particular door with all of the other toilets on this plane, so I ignore it. I hear the knock again. It's Jack. He says, "Mia, let me come in really quick. I have to go." I tell him, "I will be done in a minute." He seems to be disappointed with my reply. He says indignantly, "Mia, let me in. I want to ask you something." I was surprised. I have never had someone want to ask me something while I'm in the bathroom. I think for a few moments. I then decide to let him in. As soon as I do, he kisses me out of nowhere. He is an unbelievable kisser. His breath is still sweet despite all of the hours on the plane and our meal. I am lost in his kiss. It is just want I needed – a man who finds me sexy and who gives me his full attention. I feel Jack getting very excited. I, too, am getting aroused. He says, "I really wanted to kiss you." I just laugh. I think to myself, 'Boy, is he sweet. I like it!' Our kissing gets more intense. This is very sexy and exciting. In the back of my mind, I think: what if we get caught? I think to myself: if we are going to have sex, we'd better do it fast! Jack lifts up my skirt and slides off my panties. He smells them with a wicked smile and says, "They smell like lavender. I love the smell of good pussy." I give him a bashful smile. I am wet and ready to feel him inside of me. He makes sure we are safe first. He then bends me over the sink. I am 5'7" and he is 6'0. Our height comparison is perfect. He enters slowly inside and I lose it. It feels amazing to have this sexy ass stranger fuck me in an airplane bathroom. Talk about excitement! With his arms wrapped around me so tightly, he continually pumps me harder and harder. I am trying not to moan too loudly. We are both having a great time. I can tell he is trying not to cum too fast though. I am not anywhere near ready to cum; it usually takes me forever, which is like a cloud over my head constantly. I am disappointed that he sounds like he is about to explode at any moment. I am still trying to savor these last few moments. Jack lets out a muffled moan and pulls his dick out, rips off the condom, and cums all over my ass. It looks sexy as hell! I feel his dick throbbing against my skin. He disposes of the condom surreptitiously. We wash up as best we can. I try to fix my hair and face a bit.

There is no room in the bathroom. He opens the door first. We both exit and no one even notices. Everyone is fast asleep, even the flight attendants. Even those annoying readers and the blabbermouths were out for the count. We felt vindicated that we just had sex on a plane! What a memory and a great story to tell our friends! Despite the fun we just had, I am a little disappointed that I did not cum. Unfortunately, I am used to it. But after my self-discovery recently, I hope that will change because I know my body better.

Jack and I snuggle after our session. He seems to be very sensual and caring. He admits that he wishes that I came too. He also admits that he wanted to eat my pussy but there was no room. He jokes and tells me to lay down and spread my legs here on the seats. I tell him, "No! That would be way too risky. I would not feel comfortable doing it here". He says, "Ok. I have another idea". With my panties still off, he slides his finger into my wet pussy. It feels good. He fingers me ever so slowly. My eyes are closed and I am focusing on his sweet words and breath as he whispers in my ear. He loves my perfume and tells me how sexy and pretty I am.

He says that he loves my ass and that I turn him on so much. I love this attention! All the while, his finger continues to please me. I am starting to gyrate and fuck his finger more and more. I enjoy this tremendously. He plants kisses on my neck while his finger explores my wet spot. This goes on for quite a while. I get very excited. Despite being on a plane with nearly a hundred people in front of me, I feel myself about to cum. I feel that warm sensation approaching like before. Jack has to gently cover my mouth as I begin to moan and let out a soft yell. The orgasm is powerful - much more so than the one I gave myself back home. It goes on for a long time. It dawns on me that I must have had more than one. I am thrilled! Jack is very happy that he has pleased me and I tell him that I had a multiple orgasm. He is elated with the news. We are exhausted now – completely satisfied, but drained.

We fall asleep laying our heads together and do not wake until the sun peeks through the windows. We have our breakfast and fill out our customs forms before we land. We look at each other sheepishly, smiling about our big secret from just a few hours ago. We exchange numbers and email addresses. Even though I live in Louisiana and he lives in Atlanta, we may be able to see each other. It would be fairly easy. Soon, we land. We grab our things, retrieve our luggage together and exit the plane. We head for the customs counter. Once there, we get separated. I see him from a distance and wave. He waves back. It is sad. I hope he calls me. I will wait to hear from him. I go on my way and so does he. I will never ever forget Jack and my first overseas flight. He made it quite memorable! Ciao Giacomo, hello Europe!

# "Juliette"

## 19 July, 2013

Paris is lovely. I arrive on a sunny, Friday afternoon. Even though it is quite dirty, it is so romantic. The Eiffel Tower is breathtaking. I went to the top earlier today. I took the lift to the first floor and had some drinks, then took some photos. I thought that traveling alone would be difficult but it is quite relaxing and I am learning more and more about myself. I have met people from all over the world, and many from the States.

I proceed to the second floor of the Tower and take more photos. I look out onto the streets below and cannot believe how high up I am and I still have not made it up to the top. Instead of taking the lift to the top floor, I decide to take the stairs. Since I work out, it is not so exhausting. Once I reach the top floor, I feel such a sense of empowerment and strength. There is a bar to buy champagne and people are taking pictures. I, too, buy a glass of bubbly and ask a couple from Florida to take a few shots of me. I quickly download them to Facebook for my friends and family to see. I still have not unfriended Kenny. He will be shocked to see where I am. That will be good for him. I must admit that I want him to squirm and get a little jealous of all the fun I am having without him.

I continue on with my tour of the tower. I walk around the deck, peering onto the streets and the park below from every angle above. Responses from my posting start to pour in. All of the replies are positive; my friends are so happy for me but my parents are worried about me because I did not tell them where I was going. I just wanted to get away. I will email them my itinerary when I get back to the hotel. For now, I am free as can be. No one really knows my whereabouts or where I am headed. I prefer it that way.

Ken sends me a private message. He is astounded that I decided to travel to Europe. He wants to know who I am with, how long I am staying and if he can come and join me. I ignore him. I have nothing to say to him. Why won't he take the tart whose pussy he was slurping on? He has a lot of nerve! I would not let him touch me, see, or even talk to me. He did not appreciate me while he had me, so I know he will not appreciate me down the road. I am moving forward, not backwards. He continues to send me messages but I do not respond. I am actually enjoying this.

I finally decide to descend the Tower. Near the park, there is a merry-go-round and a Ferris wheel. I take a ride on the Ferris wheel and then buy some ice cream. I later make my way to the park and sit on the bench. I enjoy watching the people go by. I ponder where all of these people come from. They literally come from Europe, Asia, US, Africa, South America – everywhere. I hear different languages around me constantly. It's funny, being away from home, I really can tell where Americans are from – Boston area, the South, New York, Minnesota, New Orleans or out West. I speak to Americans whenever I run into them and strike up a conversation. I do not speak to people in other languages just yet; I feel shy and not really ready to be that sociable. I haven't spoken different languages in years and my confidence is not great in that area.

As I sit on the bench alone, a young girl sits next to me. I am surprised she did but I do not mind. I figure she is French. She has the "look" just like I am sure that I have the same "look" to her. She begins to speak to me in French. I am surprised. I respond to her using perfect French; she is astonished. Most Americans do not speak languages and if they do, not that well. She and I talk about the weather, France, America, politics – almost everything. Finally, I ask her, "Comment-vous appelez vous?" She replies, "Juliette". "What a lovely name", I tell her in French. She smiles. She asks me mine and I tell her, "Je m'appelle Mia". She asks me if I am "Italienne" and I tell her, "No." We acknowledge that we are both starving and she invites me to get a bite to eat with her. We take the Métro and go to a café near Notre Dame Cathedral. It is gorgeous. Even though it is night, it is beautifully lit and one can see the detail of the saints sculpted onto the church. The artwork is stunning. The detail is mesmerizing.

Juliette and I order our food. I have some beef stroganoff and she has pasta. I order the stroganoff because it reminds me of my mom. Mom makes the best

I've ever had. Anyway, the food is very good. We have some wine as well. Here I am in Paris, speaking French at a café with a new friend. Things are going way better than I ever expected.

Once in a while, I think about Jack. I wonder where he is and if he is staying near me. I wonder why he did not give me his hotel information. Maybe he is seeing someone here. After all, he did say that he comes every other year. Well, I cannot worry about it. If we are meant to meet up again, we will. I am a true believer in, 'if something is meant to be, it will be'. I quickly shift my focus back onto Juliette and our conversation, which is very interesting. I find out that she is in culinary school and works part-time as a chef at a local restaurant. Although she is very svelte, she loves to eat. She bakes and creates all types of delights. Her profession sounds very interesting. She has worked in various restaurants in Paris since she was young to gain experience. She tells me that she plans to open her own restaurant when she graduates. Her dream is to open a French restaurant in the United States. I think it is a good idea. We can always use more French restaurants in New Orleans. As we continue to chat, we keep filling our glasses with wine. I am starting to notice that Juliette is gazing into my eyes. I am not sure what is happening. All of a sudden, she seems to have an interest in me. Is it the alcohol? She did not come off that way at the park. I have never been with a woman, so maybe this is not what I think.

We leave the café and check out the entertainment outside Notre Dame. There are always performers doing different stunts throughout the day and night. It is very entertaining. We see a pair of men swallowing fire and a group of acrobats performing unbelievable stunts. I have never seen such talent. Juliette sees them all the time. She is not impressed. She passes by the Notre Dame every day. Paris for her is like New Orleans for me. New Orleans is not fascinating to me. She very patiently walks with me past all of the tourist hotspots. We later head to the Quartier Latin (Latin Quarter). It is similar to open markets back home but with the stores and restaurants lined up along narrow, cobbled stoned, hilly streets. There are tons of shops with so much merchandise and types of food. I start my shopping here at the Latin

Quarter. I love the clothes, which I cannot find back home.

We stop again and have more drinks. This time, we have margaritas. They are strong and excellent. We each have two large ones. We both get up to use the restroom and discover we cannot stand up. I was not expecting to be so tipsy. While Juliette and I are having a ball and enjoying our high, my cell phone rings. I bet I know who it is – Kenny! I pick up and listen to what he has to say. He only has a minute. He implores me take him back and pledges his undying love for me. He promises me the world. Of course, I don't believe him. This is a man who did not even care whether or not I had an orgasm. Now, he expects me to believe that he will put me first? I'm not buying it. I quickly remind him how much he likes to eat other women's pussies instead of mine. "What the fuck is up with that?" I yell at him. He has no response. At that moment, I decide just to hang up. He is not worth ruining my fun in Paris. I feel liberated. I need to disconnect from him. I did not have the chance to tell him how I feel – until then. Juliette could not understand everything that I said, but she knew I was pissed. We had a great laugh.

We each go to the restroom and then we leave. We then decide it's time to head back. I take a taxi to my hotel and she takes the Métro. I worry about her taking the train so late, but it is not like at home. People take the Métro all times of the night. But, before we go our separate ways, she gives me a kiss. I was shocked but not surprised. The alcohol made me relaxed, brave, and a little naughty and giggly. It was a soft, sweet kiss. It was respectful and sensual. I was awakened yet again. Her kisses were breezy and gentle. Juliette and I decide to sightsee tomorrow. This will be interesting!

Juliette seems to be excited to show me around the city. We get started early. We meet up at 8am. First, we go to a café for our chocolat chaud (hot chocolate) despite the fact that is in mid-summer. The French love their chocolate, whether it's candies, hot chocolate or pastries. We also have a baguette. I don't eat bread like this back home. But when in Rome, do as the Romans do, right? I always obsess about my weight like most women. But after all, I'm in Paris on vacation! To hell with my never-ending diet! Anyway, after we have our breakfast, we are off to the L'ouvre. I love art and this museum is for art lovers. We take photos by the crystal pyramid like all the other tourists. The line is long to enter into the museum. As we wait, I notice Juliette staring at me very intriguingly. I pretend not to notice. She seems to be pondering many things about me. I am faced with the fact that there is an attraction brewing between us. I am caught off guard with this situation. I have never been attracted to women. I enjoy dick very much when it's done right. Pussy doesn't do it for me. It kind of scares me. I am very neat and clean and very meticulous about my body, especially my private area. I would expect a female lover to be the same way. It's not a turn on if someone is not fresh and clean.

We finally get our tickets and begin to walk the museum. With our maps, our tour commences. There are two levels to the L'ouvre Museum. We take our time in each section. I cannot believe that I am finally here! The artwork is beautiful. We make it over to the Mona Lisa. The painting is not large at all. Most expect it to be a large, grand painting. It's not. It is about 30"x 20". There were crowds of people all trying to see it. It was a little disappointing, I must admit. Next, we visit the Venus de

Milo sculpture. It is life size and has a very interesting background. I love how our tour is a cultural and history lesson at the same time. We then head to the Egyptian area. I love Egyptian artwork and the hieroglyphics. The gold and plum colors are so beautiful. I gaze at the mummies and am amazed that these are people who lived thousands of years ago. Now, they are mummified flesh for millions to ogle upon. It's sad to me in a way – very intrusive. Their souls are not resting in peace. I have a healthy respect for karma, energy, and for those who have passed on. Juliette echoes my sentiments.

We finally finish with the L'ouvre. We then make it to the Champs Elysée. It is a long, wide street and at the end is the Arc de Triomphe. We do some shopping and have a coffee and some pastries. The food is amazing in Paris and the pastries are to die for! Everything is freshly made. The butter, milk, eggs, meat, and chocolate are high quality. The meat tastes different. The potatoes are yellowish in color and have a taste I have never had before. I will gain 10 pounds at least I am sure. Juliette is quite small despite all of this food. Most Europeans are slender. They eat well, go to the market each day and buy what they need for each meal for the day. We cannot imagine shopping that way because we buy food for a week or so and they just buy for the day.

It's time for lunch now. It's 2pm. I feel kind of uneasy. I know that things are heating up with Juliette. I just decide to take it as it comes, so-to-speak. We go to an Italian Restaurant. I get to practice my Italian. No one speaks English, only French or Italian, which is fine with me. It forces me to practice my languages more. I love Northern Italian food. It is cheesy with little to no sauce. I don't like sauce very much. Southern Italian food is tends to be very saucy – not my speed. I order the tortellini with turkey sausage and Juliette has the spaghetti al forno (baked spaghetti with cheese). We also order wine. Here we go!

As we sip on our wine, Juliette stares into my eyes very intently. I have heard that lesbian and bisexual women communicate through the eyes. It is too risky to hit on a woman without really knowing if they are into women. So, they use the eyes to see if a woman is interested. I know that if I look back at her without looking away, she will know that I am indeed interested and receptive to her advances. I have to think fast. Do I look back at her or do I look away? I decide to look away. I am not in the mood for a one-on-one lesbian encounter. I decide to keep it simple and just have a relaxing meal and enjoy my new friend's company.

Juliette does not seem to be phased by my 'disinterest'. It seems like she is used to the chase. It looks like she is up for the challenge. She is very patient and determined. I can tell. Our food comes. We both dig in and order more wine. We talk about going out later in the evening. She wants to take me to a nightclub. I think that it will be fun. We've had three to four glasses of wine and a delicious meal. We are feeling very laid back and adventurous. Lucky for us, her flat is only a few blocks away. We pay our bill and head to her apartment. I am thinking that she may try something, but I am so tired, I need to lie down and get some rest.

We get to her apartment. It is very unique and cultural. She has a lot of international art. She has traveled to many countries and has collected quite a bit of artwork. She offers me something to drink. I agree. She brings me some brandy. It's really good. She turns on some French music, which I love. Right away, she kisses me. I am shocked that she came onto me like that. I kiss her back. This time, she uses lots of tongue. I reciprocate. I am relaxed and receptive to her kisses and the attention I am getting from this beautiful French woman. I feel myself getting wet. I wonder how this can happen. I am not attracted to women but for some reason, I am to her. I guess there is always someone of the same sex who could get to us depending on the circumstances.

Juliette pulls off my blouse and begins to kiss me on my neck and caresses my breasts. My nipples are hard. I hear myself moaning. My body likes what she is doing to it. Before I even realize it, my bra is off. My large breasts are exposed with hard nipples aching to be sucked. Juliette lays me down and starts to suck on each nipple. It feels so good. The wine has me feeling so relaxed. I am ecstatic right now. I want to feel her warm mouth on my pussy now. I cannot wait. I know it is coming but she wants me to be dying for it. Her mouth moves down my middle. She gently bites my sides. She then works her way down to my inner thighs. Her sweet tongue explores my thighs so gently and lightly. I feel myself getting wetter and wetter. When is she going to go for my pussy? I want her to do it now! She knows it. I ask her to eat my pussy. She says, "Oh, I will eat this pussy alright. I am going to suck on his juicy clit until you beg me screaming to stop!" Right after she says that, her tongue begins to lick my sweet spot. It can't get any wetter. It feels unbelievable. Juliette knows what she is doing. She sucks my clit with the perfect force that sends chills through my body. Usually, it takes forever for me to cum, but not with her! I quickly feel an orgasm coming gently but very intensely. Before I know it, I cum so hard – harder than ever before. Juliette continues to voraciously eat my pussy. She is not done and the sensation is so overwhelming that I don't want her to stop. This time, she gently fingers my pussy while she hungrily slurps on my pussy juices. Could it be? I feel myself cumming again! No one has excited me so much before. To my surprise, I cum again and she continues on. At this point, I am moaning and screaming uncontrollably. My thighs are tightly wrapped around her head. She doesn't seem to mind in the least. She really knows what she is doing! I feel like it is time to reciprocate but pussy has always scared me. Despite all of this pleasure, I still wonder if she will taste good and if I will like it. I have never even been up close to one before. After all, I just had my first lesbian kiss two days ago. The idea of eating pussy was still very scary and off-putting for me.

Juliette finally comes up to my face and kisses me. To my surprise, I love the way her mouth tastes. I am tasting my own juices and I like it. It is thrilling. Kenny only ate me out once or twice. It seemed so painful to him that I just told him to come back up whenever he decided to be adventurous. It was a waste of time for both of us. I had a few other boyfriends who liked to do it but no one ever really did it quite right for me. My body is so hard to please that I think most men were just turned off by it or did not have the patience to really and truly take the time to please me. I got used to it. I got accustomed to them cumming and me not climaxing. I still always enjoyed lovemaking and if and when I had an orgasm, I was like, "great"! But, it was no big deal really if it didn't happen. I always continued to love the men that I was with. I was faithful and enjoyed them and accepted them for who they were and what they felt comfortable doing in bed.

As Juliette and I kiss and my pussy continues to throb from those two very intense orgasms, I contemplate whether or not I should go down on her. I want to but I am truly terrified. She is already very excited that she has turned me on and made me cum. I decide to take the plunge. I roll her over onto her back and begin to kiss her neck and I move down to her breasts. They are so perfect, soft and tasty. She likes feeling my mouth on them. I enthusiastically suck on them and I enjoy every minute. I like how she gets excited. I feel myself getting turned on. While I enjoy her breasts, she gyrates her hips back and forth. She wants to me to do her now. I move down and kiss her stomach and sides. I move further down and kiss her inner thighs. My eyes wander to her soft, wet spot and I take a look at what she is longing for me to devour. I kiss it gently first. She lets out a soft moan. She tastes so good and is so wet. Without ever having done this before, I start to eat Juliette's pussy as if this is a hobby of mine. My tongue explores her clit, lips, and hole so thoroughly. I am proud of myself. I am pleasing a woman! I never thought in a million years that I would ever do this and enjoy it but I love it!! Juliette is enjoying my tongue and I love the way her pussy feels in my mouth. Like she did to me, I gently fuck her pussy with my finger as I eat her. She loves it. Her body begins to shudder. She is cumming and it will be intense. I can tell. She talks dirty to me, "Mia, you eat my pussy so fucking good, baby! It feels so good! I'm gonna squirt in your face!" I think to myself: 'Squirt? Oh, shit!' I have heard of women squirting but I cannot believe that my first one-on-one lesbian experience is with a fucking squirter! There is no time to get scared. I am into this and I am taking everything as it comes – so-to-speak. Before I know it, I feel this warm liquid squirt forcefully into my mouth! It has a sweet taste to it. I quickly move my head away for a second; I want to see her squirt in the air. As I move away and she squirts, I catch a little bit in my mouth and all over my face. This is fucking crazy! I dive back into her pussy and continue on. Juliette is out of control with pleasure. She wants me to keep going and I am still totally into it. I suck on her clit the way she did mine and she cums again, squirting in my mouth. 'Shit, this is unbelievable,' I think to myself. It is ironic that I longed for Ken to go down on me and here I am going down on a woman and loving every minute of it. How could he pass up on this? Damn, he had some issues! I guess it was okay to go down on other women but not me. Maybe he wanted to feel like he was controlling me and keeping me in check.

Juliette rolls me over onto my back. She starts to grind on my pussy with hers. I heard about lesbians 'bumpin coochie' as another alternative to reach orgasm but I never thought that it felt so good, but it does. Our two wet pussies forcefully and quickly grind against each other. We moan and groan heavily in delight. Our hands are wrapped around each other's bodies. Our soft breasts are pressed together. Her warm body feels unbelievable against mine. We exchange sensual kisses. The kisses are warm, slow, and other times, they are hard and passionate. This sex is unreal – probably the best that I have ever had.

After our incredible session, we lay exhausted from intense pleasure, breathing hard, lying on saturated sheets and wetness all over our faces and bodies. Out of breath,

Juliette tells me how incredible she thinks our lovemaking was. I was happy to hear that she was so pleased with my performance and that she had no idea that I am still a novice. She, however, is an expert. She is bisexual. She enjoys men just as much as she likes women. She does not let a person's gender dictate her attraction. I think that is an enticing way to live life and handle relationships, especially as a woman. Society is getting more and more tolerant of bisexual woman. It is no longer taboo if a woman is bi. In fact, most men find it extremely hot. I then think to myself, 'am I bisexual?' If a woman can eat pussy excitedly, then I think it is safe to say that she is bi or even gay. Not everyone can eat pussy and suck on boobs. Kissing a woman is one thing, but eating pussy takes it all to another level.

It is not long before we fall asleep holding each other. Even though I barely know this woman, what we just shared was so intimate - more intimate than any other sex I have ever had. I had multiple orgasms, and this woman squirted in my face and mouth! That is about as intimate as it gets!

My stay in Paris is coming to an end. Juliette and I continue to spend time together. We finish touring the city, going to cafés, and dinner. I love spending time with her. I am impressed with her knowledge of various cultures, the city of Paris, and France's history. She turns me on in more ways than one.

On this day, we go to Palace of Versailles. It is a massive palace located in Versailles, which is about 20 minutes on the outskirts of Paris. King Louis and his wife, Marie Antoinette, and their daughter lived in this monstrosity. The gardens are vast and magnificent. Walls throughout the residence are made with gold. There are hundreds of rooms (700) throughout the palace. Despite the fact that it's quite crowded, we still enjoy ourselves. The walk through the gardens is peaceful. It is hard to believe that this property has been around for centuries and such tragic events took place here during the French Revolution. This place has to be haunted at night. Its owners were both beheaded after all.

I am not looking forward to saying goodbye to Juliette. Even though we are not long-standing lovers, I feel like this past week, we were. We had fun dates, great meals and awesome sex. In some relationships, they end without people seeing it coming like with Ken. Other times, we end it ourselves and have control of the situation. In this case, our friendship will be forced to end because I am leaving Paris for Amsterdam. We discussed the possibility of her joining me there for a few days, but she cannot. She is unable to take off from work. I am disappointed but I guess it is for the best. After all, she lives 5,000 miles away. The phones bills and traveling back and forth would cost a fortune. Would I really want to have a long distance lesbian relationship anyway? It sounds exhausting to try to keep such a relationship going. We do agree to try and visit at least once a year and to keep in touch via Facebook and email. No matter what happens with each other and or with other people, we decide to keep the friendship going and if any 'benefits' continue to occur now and then, then so be it.

During my last night in Paris, we go to the Eiffel Tower and have dinner in the restaurant on the first floor. The view is spectacular and it is such an elegant place to dine. It is very romantic as well. We use lots of eye contact unlike our first date when I was so nervous. I am attracted to her and not afraid of her like before. We take the lift to the top of the tower for the last time. We have some champagne and enjoy the breathtaking view. It is very crowded on deck and filled with mostly Americans. I hear English widely spoken. It feels like I am back home in America.

Juliette and I stand close to each other, taking in the spectacular view before us. We hug and smile at each other. We know this date is very special. My trip to Paris is coming to an end. I share with Juliette, "J'adore Paris et je suis très heureuse que j'ai passé ma vacances avec toi. Merci, Juliette. Tu es une bonne amie." (I adore Paris and I am very happy that I spent my vacation with you. Thank you, Juliette. You are a great friend.) Juliette is moved by my words. She replies, "Pas problem, ma Cherie." (No problem, my dear.)

We hold hands and descend the Tower and head to her apartment. We don't care if people notice our public display of affection. Unbeknownst to me, Juliette has some tasty plans for us tonight. We have eaten wonderful food our entire time in Paris but today Juliette wants us to be naughty. She brings out this amazing strawberry shortcake, which happens to be one of our favorites. Juliette has a huge piece for us to share. It looks amazing. She gets a fork, cuts a piece and feeds it to me. It tastes so good. I close my eyes and smile as I eat it. The cake melts in my mouth. The whipped cream is unreal. I take the fork and feed her a piece too, smiling at her all the while. I give her another piece but I purposely feed it to her messily. I want to see her luscious tongue lick the cream off of those sexy lips of hers. I am in a trance staring at her tongue as she licks away the whipped cream. It's my turn again. She feeds me some more cake. This time I get a mouthful of juicy, syrupy strawberries. The strawberry juice drips along the side of my mouth. Juliette sensually licks it off of me. She gives me another piece of cake with lots of whipped cream. It gets all over my mouth. She kisses me and slowly licks it off for me. I moan as she licks away. I take my fingers, dip them in the whipped cream and stick my fingers in her mouth. She licks and sucks away. Chills are going through my body while she sucks my fingers. Juliette's eyes are closed. She is totally focused on sucking on my fingers so good. She takes the cake and leaves the kitchen. I follow her to the bedroom. She lays the cake on the nightstand. She grabs me and pulls me close to her and begins to kiss me so sweetly. I enjoy her warm, sweet smelling body tremendously. She slowly undresses me and lies me on the bed. She opens my legs wide and smears some cream on my shaved pussy so slowly. It drives me insane. She likes seeing my pussy covered in whipped cream. Very slowly, she licks the cream away. I moan as she enjoys her 'pussy with cream' treat. I tell her that I want to suck her nipples. I get some whipped cream and smear some on her breasts. I love having her round, small breasts in my mouth while I feel her nipples getting harder and harder as I gently bite and forcefully suck on them. Juliette goes wild. We enjoy playing with each other with the cream. One at a time, we take turns spreading whipped cream on each other. Luckily, I enjoy Juliette first; she tastes so sweet to me. Feeling her creamy clit on my tongue and listening to her moans, I get very wet and so excited. I can tell she is about to cum. I brace myself for the squirt. I hear her scream, "Je viens, Mia! Veux-tu que je viennes dans ta bouche?" (I'm cumming, Mia. Do you want me to cum in your mouth?) So turned on, I whisper with a mouth full of pussy, "Oui, baby. Viens dans ma bouche." (Yes, baby. Cum in my mouth!") The combination of her squirt and the whipped cream tastes so good. Her squirt has the most wonderful, sweet taste. After she cums, she is determined to make me cum too. Delirious from devouring her sweet box, Juliette flips me over and dives down to my pussy. I am exhausted from my hard work but I long for my turn now. As Juliette pleases me, I hump her face really enthusiastically. My hands are tightly grasped around her ears. I can't help it. It feels so good. I feel my orgasm cumming. I hump her tongue so hard. My body feels so hot. It is a long, deep orgasm. I scream out her name so loudly – "Juliette! That feels so good, baby!"

This feeling is euphoric. We have a fabulous time during my last night in Paris. The next morning Juliette takes me to airport. I am on way to Amsterdam – the exquisitely old city on water. Adieu for now, Juliette.

# "Amsterdam"

## 23 July, 2013

On the plane ride to Amsterdam, I cannot help but think about Jack. Every time I take a plane ride, I will think of our passionate, fun rendezvous. I have met two adventurous people. Each time, I was minding my own business and not thinking about meeting someone new. Why does this keep happening to me? I hope things slow down. I still have to deal with Ken when I get home. I didn't really handle with the situation as I should have. I know I will have to totally cut him loose or give him another chance. Part of me feels like we spent so many years together, that maybe we should try again, if he is willing to work on his sexual weaknesses. I realize that I still love him, unfortunately…

I land at the Schipol Airport. It is a beautiful, large airport. I catch a cab to my hotel. It is about 15 minutes from the airport, and just around the corner from the Anne Frank House. Amsterdam is a lovely, old, scenic town on water. Most people get around either by bike or ferry. Some people do have cars, but that's rare and those people tend to be very wealthy.

I hear Dutch spoken all around me. Even though most Dutch people speak English, they tend not to when they are in each other's company. I don't speak the language, so I feel a little isolated. I now wish that I had learned at least a little bit with a CD. I feel very vulnerable not being able to communicate in Dutch. Thanks goodness most of them do speak English though!

Once I arrive at my hotel, I take a much needed hot bath and just relax. I feel myself falling asleep in the warm, soft, oily, scented water. The water is so soothing; it makes me feel so much better. I have not really had any quiet time alone since I've been in Europe. I was with Juliette my entire stay. We had a blast but I did need to spend some time by myself to regroup. I have to make sure that I do that on this part of my trip.

After my amazing bath, I take a much needed nap. I just want to relax without having to worry about anyone inviting me here and or wanting to take me there. I am on my own schedule now and I love it!

I later wake up from my nap. I am ready to take a tour with the hotel. On this excursion, we will travel to the countryside to see the tulip gardens and the windmills. The bus ride is a good hour away. The entire ride is beautiful flatland for miles and miles. When we arrive at the gardens, the flowers are breathtaking. There are so many colors and arrangements throughout the gardens. The windmills are off in the distance but they are huge. It was a great tour that ended with an interesting lunch. The Dutch diet is pretty different from the American one. First of all, they love buttermilk. The name alone to me sounds disgusting. Apparently, they drink this three to four times per day. They drink tall 12 oz. glasses of this thick, creamy, yellowish milk. If that was not bad enough, lunch was a buffet. One of most common components of breakfast in some European countries is raw bacon! It is kept on the steam table uncooked. It is fatty and soft, but served very warm. 'How can people eat this', I think to myself. The thought of eating raw bacon makes me sick to my stomach. But I remember that when I am traveling, it is imperative to assimilate to the 'new' culture. We have to leave the

American culture at home and experience everything the new culture has to offer. I continue to study all of the strange dishes on the steam table. I see creamed beef, which I don't like at all. I see sausages and boiled eggs. There is oatmeal and off to the side I see some bread. I go with the boiled eggs, sausage and bread. I think my choices are safe. I sit alone and keep my fingers crossed that I don't have any issues from the food. I have heard stories of people getting sick because of the change in diet or the water. I am very careful about what I put in mouth. I am willing to try new foods, but I don't want to have to return home and cut my trip short because I ate something that I knew I had no business eating.

As I am eating, a young man comes over to me. He asks, "Is anyone sitting here?" I think to myself, 'All of these tables here? Why does he want to sit next to me? I want some peace for once – no interaction!' I don't let on that I am perturbed. I relent and tell him, "No. It's all yours." He thanks me. When I look down at his plate and see the raw bacon, I'm done! I am like, 'Lord, please let this man finish fast before I get sick'.

I knew he was Dutch from what was on his plate. I naïvely thought that there were not many black people in the Netherlands, but I was wrong. Holland is loaded with black people who migrate back and forth from the Dutch colonies in the Caribbean and Suriname in South America. I am quite intrigued after seeing this tall, 6'6" black Dutchman. He has a rich caramel complexion with a tint of red. His hair is sandy brown and he has green eyes. I am starting not to pay attention to what is on his plate. So I reel it back in and try to learn more about him. He asks me where I am from. I tell him, "New Orleans". He says, "I hear New Orleans is a beautiful city with great food." I tell him, "Yes. Our food is definitely some of the best in the world. You should come and visit sometime. You would love it!" He agrees. I curiously ask him, "What's your name?" He tells me, "Floyd". "What a plain, Anglo name", I tell him. He says, "I was named after my grandfather who was from Guyana. My family is from Suriname but my grandfather came to my country from Guyana before I was born. My parents named me after him. He spoke perfect English, Dutch, and Spanish. Most people in Suriname speak Spanish because it's in

South America. We learned Spanish in grade school. It was a requirement." I am attracted to his background in languages. Unlike me, he inherited his multilingualism as a young child, but I chose to pursue it.

Even though we are enjoying our conversation, I try not to watch him eat. The buttermilk and raw bacon are truly making me feel sick. I cannot take this cuisine. Luckily, the interesting conversation and his mesmerizing good looks keep me from peering at his food every 10 seconds.

"Well, it is time for me to meet back up with my group, Floyd. It was a pleasure meeting and talking to you." He looks at me curiously and says, "Do you really think that I was not going to ask to show you around Amsterdam?" Stunned and taken aback, I reply, "That would be great." Floyd reassures me that he will be a perfect gentleman and I will have so much more fun seeing the city with him than with a tour group. I agree. I am just concerned that he will try to make a move. I have certainly had enough action to last me for the rest of the year! I really don't think I can take another lover. I can't. I hope I am not overreacting.

I take Floyd up on his offer on one condition: that I go back to the hotel with the tour bus and meet him there at 9pm for dinner. He agrees. I do not feel comfortable riding with him in his car back to my hotel. That is not an option.

When I get back to my hotel, I change clothes. I don't wear anything sexy. In fact, I dress kind of plain and simple. I put on some loose jeans, a button down shirt, a sweater and a jacket along with some cowboy boots. My makeup is light - barely visible - and my jewelry is minimal. Much to my surprise, Floyd is turned on by that! He does not hesitate to tell me, "Mia, you look really sexy. I love when a woman embraces her natural beauty and does not overdo makeup and dress tastelessly". I think to myself, 'Damn!!'

I go with the flow. We start our outing on foot. We walk around the area. We finally get to a restaurant. Most of the clientele are young people. The smell of marijuana is evident. I knew this would be an issue, but I pretend that it does not bother me. I am tempted to smoke a little something, but I don't know Floyd, and therefore, I don't trust him yet. Since I am here alone, I can't be too careful.

We get a table and look at the menus. There is a section just for hash alone. Geez! I keep it simple and just order some fish and chips. That seems to be the generic European dish that never disappoints. I can only wonder what Floyd wants to order. Thankfully, he goes with a burger and fries. I am relieved.

As we wait for our food, we inquire a little bit more about each other. He asks, "Are you married, have kids or both?" I tell him, "No. I am single and with no children. This is not how I planned my life but this is my current situation. And you?" He says that he is divorced with one daughter; she's 17. I have no idea how old Floyd is and I know that he doesn't know my age either, so I just keep it like that. He may or may not like a woman in her mid-40's. Many men prefer women younger for some odd reason.

The couple next to us is smoking pot. It is really strong and I can tell it is good shit! I slowly take in the lovely marijuana aroma. Floyd is used to this. He has been around drugs his whole life. Whenever the family would go out to dinner, sometime his parents would order something 'fun' and other times, they would not. I am so tempted to order something, but I decide not to. Luckily, our food arrives. It looks really good. Floyd and I continue our conversation over this delicious food. He notices my eyes and smile. He makes several comments. Despite it all, I always enjoy compliments from men. This quasi attraction between Floyd and me is partly because of our nationalities and the stereotypes we both believed about Blacks in the US and Holland. I am the first Black American woman that he has met and gotten to know. It doesn't sound like he is willing to let me go on my merry way and I am not so sure that I want him exit so quickly either.

After dinner, he takes me for a walk past the Red Light District. I have heard about it often, but seeing it is really something. We see beautiful women in these large, glass encased rooms. The district is along a small walkway. People walk along the walkway and look at the women behind the glass. They are seductively dressed, hoping that someone will ring the buzzer for some fun. I am amazed at these women and how they are willing to give their bodies to total strangers, who, in many cases, do not speak their language or their other adopted languages. We continue to walk and we go to a café. We have a seat and get a drink. I need one after that steamy Red Light experience. I was not attracted to any of the women, but there was a little bit of sexual tension between Floyd and me. How could there not be? We are in a sexy city where pot is at our fingertips if we so choose. While we are having our drinks, our conversation got a little deep. Floyd wants to know why I never married or had kids. I tell him about Ken and what happened. I don't go into detail but Floyd can tell there is more to the story. He prods. I finally tell him how I followed Ken to San Francisco and caught him going down on another woman. Floyd got a kick out of the story. I had no idea why. It is still pretty upsetting for me. Floyd tells me that he caught his daughter's mom in bed with her ex. He says that they were having some problems in their relationship and she took it upon herself to call up her ex. It did not take long for them to start a hot and heavy affair. One day, Floyd came home from work early, and caught them in the kitchen. He saw his wife in the air with her legs wrapped around some tall, blond guy's back. He was fucking the shit out of her. She was yelling so loudly that she didn't even hear him come into the house. It got really bad. He started to beat up the guy. The wife started crying. Floyd demanded that she choose who she wanted to be with, but she couldn't choose. She wanted both, apparently. Floyd explained that he could not share his wife with someone else. He told me that he could share a girlfriend possibly, but not his wife and mother of his child. I was shocked that he said that he could share a girlfriend. But Europeans, in general, are a lot more open-minded than the typical American. I am reminded of this each day I visit this magical place.

Now Floyd and I have something in common: cheating spouses who we actually caught in the act. This, believe it or not, bonds us together. We talk about our relationships and what we did wrong and all that we did right. It is a fun conversation, but painful at the same time. Even though Floyd broke up with his ex-years ago, it still bothers him. Maybe if he had not caught her in the act in such an explosive situation, he would not be so hurt. Same thing for me: the way I saw Ken with that woman was such a crazy visual. It haunts me sometimes, but then I get angry because he never did that to me for whatever reason. And I was supposed to be his partner forever, so I thought.

After we finish with our drinks, Floyd and I head to a park. It is well lit and there are other couples there. It is at that moment that I realize he wants to kiss me. I let it happen. His lips are so soft. He has a pearly white smile and sweet breath. His hands are perfectly manicured and he has a sexy, alluring scent too. He passes the hygiene test! After the kiss, he asks me, "Do you have any fetishes, Mia?" I think for moment. I tell him, "No, I don't think so. Why? Do you?" He smiles and says, "Yes. I like ass". I'm like, "Okay. Lots of guys are into big butts. That's no big deal." He says, "No. I am really into ass. I love giving anal and I love receiving and doing analingus." For me – blank stare. That is kind of a lot to take in. We have all had close encounters with the butt. Every once in a while after a ton of drinks, lots of wet, juicy sex, the dick might end up in there and it can be a lot of unexpected, hot fun. But what he is talking about is totally different. In any event, I don't worry about it because he and I just met and I have no plans to do anything with him. I just respond, "That's interesting. You're the first person I've met who has an anal fetish." He is all smiles and quite proud of his obsession. I really don't know how to take this information. I consider myself a fairly open-minded person, but this seems a bit strange to me. Nevertheless, I won't let this information deter me from having fun and getting to know him better. I am very conscious of my ass now. I know that he is watching my every move and gazing at it every chance that he gets. That turns me on. Even though I have always gotten attention over my butt, this takes things to a whole new level. I imagine he would like to do things to my ass that I never even thought of.

It's a perfect night for a ferry cruise. We board the next boat and cruise along one of Amsterdam's dozens of canals. All of the houses that line these canals are beautifully lit; it looks like a postcard. I am in awe. I catch Floyd looking at me and smiling. I think he really likes me - not just for my butt. I do find him attractive as well. I try not to make too much of it. I just want to have fun. What goes on in Europe stays in Europe, huh? I decide that even though I am not terribly proud of my adventures these past few weeks, I have had a wonderful, unforgettable time. I still have a fair amount of time left in Europe and I will just go with the flow and try not to worry about what I should or should not do. With that said, once our ferry cruise is over, I am tired and tell Floyd that I think it is time for me to turn in. He is disappointed but he understands. He walks me back to the lobby of my hotel and kisses me on the forehead. He leaves me his cell number, email address, and his full name for me to friend him on Facebook and follow him on Instagram and Twitter. I know he likes me now. Most men would not have given me so much contact information. I give him a hug. I appreciate that he has not asked me to come up to my room. We say goodbye and agree to meet tomorrow. As I head back to my room, although I am tired, I cannot help but think about Floyd's admission. I am definitely intrigued by it. I take a shower and get into bed. My mind starts to race about what sex would be like with Floyd. I close my eyes and imagine being in bed with a man who is not 'afraid' of eating my ass out, but whom absolutely loves and prefers that over eating pussy. My dreams are quite vivid that night and I could not wait to see Floyd the next day!

He picks me up for breakfast. I do not want to eat the food in the hotel. I want to try a café instead. Again, the food there is 'safe'. I have never eaten so many pastries and breads in my life but that is what is available, so I just make the most of it. I enjoy my coffee and hot chocolate along with some bread most mornings and I don't feel any guilt. These types of pastries pretty much are non-existent back home. We have our own goodies, but the ones in Europe are undeniably unique and a constant treat.

I ask Floyd how it is that he is able to hang out with me and not work. He tells me that he works with his family's business so he has a lot of flexibility. He basically lives a comfortable life. That is a plus. There is nothing worse than dating someone who is irresponsible with money. At this stage in my life, I prefer to be with someone who can take me out once in a while and show me a good time without worrying about how the outing will be paid for.

After breakfast, Floyd takes me to the Anne Frank House and then to the Van Gogh Museum. I enjoy both places a lot. Our touring reminds me of my short time with Juliette. Floyd has literally taken me to all of the most popular sites in Amsterdam. He then takes me on a train ride to Rotterdam. There, we will enjoy a music festival. I have heard that Rotterdam is an amazing place; it is very similar to Philadelphia in that there is a very large black population and is full of culture. At the festival, people are grilling, enjoying music, smoking various things – having a great time. I am stunned that everyone in attendance is black! I think to myself, 'Where did so many black people come from?' They are all speaking Dutch. I don't hear one world of English. Floyd is great with making me feel comfortable. He explains what is going on here in there. He knows so many people; he introduces me to a few of his friends that he runs into. Most of them speak very good English; others not so much. It is okay. I love this experience and I enjoy watching Floyd hang in a different setting. He can adapt in any situation, which I find sexy. It is a talent that everyone cannot master.

After eating some unbelievable BBQ, meeting dozens of people and resisting the temptation to smoke the pot that everyone around us is enjoying, we decide to leave. While on the train, Floyd asks me: "Do you want to see where I live?" I say, "Sure" without hesitation. I am rather curious at this point. Once we get off the train, we catch a ferry. The ride is relaxing and I notice that we are passing through a fancier part of town. We get off at an early stop. There is this block of exquisite houses along the canal. I imagine that any homes alongside the water are quite expensive. As we approach his home, he knows almost every person we see. I get the impression he has lived here a long time and people know him from his prominent family. We finally arrive to his home. As Floyd opens the door to his house, I am preparing myself for what I am about to see. I expect to see a glamorous place; I don't. His house is just like all of the other Dutch houses – plain, empty, very basic. Wow! I must admit, this is a big disappointment. His place is immaculate. It is bright with wood floors. There is barely any furniture. There is some artwork hung on the walls here and there. The walls are painted with various warm colors, which adds a little character to the place, which it desperately needs. It is obvious that he has lived alone for a long time; his home does not have a woman's touch at all. He gives me a tour. I finally get to see the bedroom. I'm simply amazed. He has a queen-sized bed, a nightstand and a dresser. That's it despite the fact that his bedroom is huge. We go back out into the living room. He offers me a drink. We have some vodka. He turns on some great music and heats up some tapas for us. I love tapas. I just hope they are not too bizarre. Lucky for me they are simple and recognizable: mozzarella sticks, clam strips, and potato skins. I am thrilled!

I ask him, "Why are you single. You are a handsome man, intelligent, business savvy. What's going on?" He tells me, "I have to be careful with who I date. Everyone in the area knows my family and I never know who likes me for me and not the family fortune. For this reason, I decided not to have more children. My former girlfriends always tried to get pregnant on me, so I had to be very careful. It gets exhausting having to be so aware all of the time." I feel sorry for Floyd. He wants to date and have someone special but it sounds like people are vicious, so it is safer for him to stay to himself and just date here and there on a non-serious basis. He is a great guy with a warm personality. He would make a great boyfriend or husband for someone.

I appreciate that Floyd has opened up to me. I get the impression that he does not do this often. I guess because I am from out-of-town and he may not see me again, he feels comfortable sharing his feelings with me. I am 'safe', so-to-speak. I am glad that I can lend an ear to hear his frustrations. He tells me that his daughter lives with her mom nearby and that he sees her often. She is off to college soon and wants to go to London to study. He tells me that she speaks very good English, Dutch, German, and French. I am sure she is a smart girl and probably quite beautiful, tall and model-like.

As Floyd and I share our stories, the vodka is starting to take effect on both of us. I can tell it has been a while since he has been alone with a woman. He seems a little nervous and shy, which surprises me. I think he realizes that he can trust me. I notice that he begins to look me in my eyes more and more. I look back at him with a smile to reassure him that I am receptive to a kiss. Soon, he moves in and gives me a slow, warm, sensual kiss. He is a wonderful kisser. He gives me another and we embrace. Eventually, we are laying down on his couch. His tall, strong body is on top of mine. I enjoy having a man on top of me – a kind, caring one. In the back of my mind, I remember that Floyd is an ass man. I don't know what to expect. I wonder what is on his mind. What does he want to do with me? I dismiss those thoughts and just enjoy the moment. I am relaxed and I trust him. He has been the perfect gentleman these past few days and I appreciate that so much.

Our kissing gets more intense, more passionate. I can now feel his manhood pressing against me. His size is overwhelmingly perfect! He lifts off my blouse and looks down at my breasts hidden away by my lacy pink bra. My dark, hard nipples peak through and entice him. He starts to kiss and lick my neck, which is a major turn on for me. Instantly, I get very wet and excited. He notices the change in my body and the moaning begins. His lips move down to my breasts. He licks them through my bra very sensually and begins to bite them ever so gently. The sensation is driving me wild. He eventually takes off my bra and my large breasts pop out, anxious to be licked and sucked on. He doesn't disappoint. He sucks on my nipples so perfectly. He seems to be a breast man too! Things heat up even more. I take off his shirt and observe his tight, sexy abs. What a pleasant surprise! He then works off my skirt. I am left with my panties on. He rolls me onto my stomach. 'Here we go', I think to myself. While I am lying on my stomach, he begins to gently bite my butt cheeks through my panties. No one has ever done this to me before but I love it. I love the sensation of his teeth lightly biting me. He slowly pulls down my panties. He resumes licking and biting my cheeks. I am reeling from the sensation. He asks me to get on my knees. I comply. Once my phat ass is directly in his face, his tongue licks my asshole very slowly. He moans as his tongue explores my asshole. The feeling is so warm and soothing. It is so different from cunnilingus. I don't want him to stop and neither does he. I then feel his tongue enter inside my hole. How is this possible! He knows what he is doing. His warm tongue methodically enters inside my hole and moves about within that small, tight, warm area. His finger then travels onto my clit. He quickly caresses it while his tongue tantalizes my tight, taboo, wet spot. The feeling is overwhelming. His tongue does not tire; he continues on for what seems like an hour. He was not joking; he really does have an ass fetish. He eventually turns me over onto my back and starts to eat my pussy. Again, his tongue is so talented. I love the warm feeling of his tongue sucking and licking my clit. He then slowly slides his finger into my pussy while he slurps on my juices. The feeling is amazing. If he keeps this up, I will cum for sure. My body is getting hot and starting to slightly sweat from the intense tongue pleasing. I sweetly grab his head, holding his ears and fuck his tongue. He doesn't mind. My juices are streaming all over his face and onto the bed; it is completely saturated under me. This is unreal. I feel an orgasm cumming. I am sure to let him know. His tongue eagerly pleases me even more. I scream out his name as my thighs tighten around his head. I let out a load cry in delight. My pussy throbs from so much intense oral pleasure. I am ready to do him now. I still have not had a really good look at it. I hope it is not too big. I know that sounds odd, but if he is too big, that can be a little daunting. My hand reaches down to feel his member. Just like I thought, it is long, thick, and very hard. I will have my work cut out for me. I roll him over onto his back. I plant sensual kisses all over his lips and face. I enjoy tasting my own sweet juices on him. I then work my way to his neck, chest, and stomach. I then travel down to his dick, planting slow kisses. Once Floyd can no longer wait to feel my warm, wet mouth surround his rock hard dick, I begin to suck on it and he is a mouthful for sure. I do the best that I can. I please him with my mouth and tongue and he seems to enjoy it. I think it has been a while since he has felt this pleasure. He is very loud and can barely contain himself. I am glad that I am able to make him feel some well-deserved pleasure. I am under the impression that he will want his happy ending orally, but he doesn't. He reaches for a condom and some KY jelly. I'm like, 'Oh shit. Is he for real?' I know what the KY is for. He resumes kissing me and says, "Is it ok if we do anal?" I say, "Well, I have only done it once and it was by accident." He tells me, "Don't worry. I am really good at it and it will not hurt you at all. I promise." I believe what he says. I have no idea how he will make that happen, but I do trust him. He squeezes the gel onto my asshole. He does this very slowly and sensually. I am lying on my back and watch him as he does this. He continues until the gel begins to become warm. It is very soothing. The expression on his face as he smoothes the warm gel on my tight spot is total excitement; he can barely contain himself. I still am not sure how this will turn out. But again, I trust him. I watch him as he puts on the condom. His dick is very long, thick, and hard. I can't imagine how in the hell he thinks that thing will go into my asshole, but I will soon find out. He tells me, "Relax. I got you." My pussy is still so wet from our session. The KY just makes me wetter and more ready for this anal play. I feel the tip begin to tease my tight opening. He slowly and gently works it in more and more and he is right - it doesn't hurt. It's not long before he is going in and out of me, and it feels good. It feels warm and relaxing. I am so surprised. He knows what he is doing. He is enjoying this so much. I can tell. His body is shuddering and he is moaning intensely. He keeps saying, "Mia, it feels so good and tight. Are you ok? Does it feel ok, baby?" I tell him, "Yes. It feels good. Keep going.

I'm okay." He is delighted by my response. He continues on for a while. He asks me to do it doggie style. I am ok with him on top but, I am not so sure how it will feel doggie style. Nonetheless, I am willing to give it a try. He gently pulls it out and it hurts just a little bit. I get on my knees. He gets more lube and smoothes it on my hole once again. Very slowly, he enters back inside me. Strangely, I cannot wait for him to put it back it. I like the warm feeling. I need my hole to be filled again, as odd as that sounds. He resumes pumping my ass. It feels soothing in a strange way. I am so impressed with his skills. I never would have thought that I would enjoy anal and analingus so much, but I do.

I know that Floyd will be cumming soon but I, too, feel like an orgasm is possible for me. Floyd begins to fondle my nipples as he pumps me. That extra stimulation seems to be what I need to possibly cum. I concentrate on his dick going in and out of me. It is gooey and warm down there. I feel myself cumming. It is not a big, powerful orgasm but a smaller, reverberating one. The sensation is totally different. This orgasm creeps up on me and I let out a very low moan. It ripples through my body with strong waves unlike any other one that I have had before. Floyd is happy that I came. He now works my hole and little harder. Still, it doesn't hurt. I actually like feeling him pumping me a little harder now. I have gotten used to the sensation. I want him to keep going. After a while, he cums too but his orgasm is really powerful and long lasting. His body shudders as he lets out such a loud groan. It is unbelievable. We are both worn out. Anal takes a lot out of a person. We lay there for a moment but I need to take a shower. I am a clean freak and I always need to shower, but especially after this. I ask to use his shower and he tells me, "Sure". He shows me where the bathroom is and he turns the water on for me. He gets me a towel and soap. I ask him for a washcloth and he does not know what that is. I tell him, "It's a tiny towel-like cloth that we use to put soap in and then wash our bodies." He says, "We don't use these things in Europe. We just use our hands and soap." Wow! The cultural differences can be mind blowing at times. I just make do with my hands. I desperately want to clean myself thoroughly but it doesn't look like I will be able to do that. I will make the best of it.

When I get out of the shower, I smell something cooking. I am curious what Floyd is making but at the same time, I am a little nervous. To my surprise, he has prepared some breakfast sausage and with crêpes and coffee. Breakfast looks and tastes delicious. While we eat, I notice Floyd smiling and staring at me. I can tell he wants to say something. He asks me, "So, what did you think about last night?" I tell him, "It was incredible. I was totally at ease and relaxed. I was really surprised. It felt good and it wasn't painful at all." I was curious as to why he likes anal so much because it is a lot work and it does not always go well with everyone. It can also be viewed as risky for a variety of reasons: not everyone is super clean, it can be painful during and/or after sex and it can be a turn off for either partner if things go horribly wrong.

He tells me that the ass is intimate. It tends to be unchartered territory for most and he likes being the one who ventures to that 'untouched' area. He explains that it is tight, sexy, and pure to him. He likes to watch and experience the unique sensation women feel when his warm, wet tongue and penis venture into such a private, taboo place on their bodies. He explains that anal orgasms are very deep and reverberating. He gets a thrill from helping women achieve such pleasure. I ask him how he developed his interest and he told me that when he was an adolescent, whenever he would see attractive women, his eyes always went straight to their backsides. If a woman had a full, round ass, he was sexually awakened. But, if he saw women with flat, unattractive butts, he was completely turned off. He said his friends were into boobs and pretty faces. He says that he felt weird because his attention was directed in an area that was not as popular. Boys looked at girls' butts but Floyd knew early on that he wanted to explore their butts, not just gaze at them and squeeze them.

I asked him to tell me about his first sexual experience. He smiles with delight. I can tell this will be a very interesting story. Floyd shares with me that he had a French teacher in junior high school. She was beautiful; she was biracial with blond hair and blue eyes. Her dad's family was from Aruba; when they came to the Netherlands, he met her mom. He was mesmerized by her beauty. She had strong European facial features but had the sultry body of a curvy, black woman. This teacher had full breasts, a small waist, wonderful hips, and a beautiful, full ass.

Floyd loved going to school every day. He looked forward to seeing his lovely teacher every morning. She spoke beautiful Dutch and French. He got all A's in class. It was with her that he would discover his intrigue with derrières, but it was not unusual to him. Instead, it was beautiful and ultimately sexy. Floyd found himself masturbating at night thinking about his teacher. He envisioned her riding his dick with her back facing him. He pictured her phat, light, caramel-colored ass riding up and down on his shaft so vividly.

After countless dreams and fantasies about her, he realized that he had to do something to relieve his sexual tension. A relationship with his teacher was out of the question, unfortunately. Luckily, there was an older classmate who expressed quite a strong interest in him. He never really thought about fooling around with her until his passion began to get out of control for his teacher. He was afraid that he would do or say something foolish in class.

His schoolmate, Claudia, was a junior and Floyd was in 8th grade. She was attracted to him because of his height. At the tender age of 14, Floyd was already 6'2", which is not so unusual for Dutch people. She was 6'0. Her family was well off and they went away to different European cities each weekend. She invited Floyd countless times over to her house to 'hang out'. He finally agreed. They made plans for a Friday night. She ordered take out for dinner. Floyd arrived around 8:00 in the evening. They had a candlelit dinner and wine, which is not unusual for teenagers in Europe. After dinner, they watched a movie. Claudia was very aggressive. Five minutes into the movie, she kissed him passionately using her tongue quite generously. Floyd was impressed with her lingual skills. She then grabbed his hard, large dick. He was overwhelmed with excitement. Claudia then pulled out his manhood and started to blow him slowly. He tells me that he came almost instantly. She was disappointed but not surprised. Her next idea definitely gave Floyd pause: she ordered him to lie on his back and move down on the bed. To his amazement, she then climbed onto his face. She told him to use his tongue to please her. As she moved back and forth on his tongue, Floyd got a taste of her asshole.

For some reason, that hole excited him more than her pussy did. He was in awe of this warm, wet mound on top of his face, completely submerging him. He got turned on by Claudia's moans and groans. All the while, he was more and more turned on by the sensation of licking her asshole. He noticed that the more he licked her there, the more she went crazy. He did not hesitate to gently slide his tongue into it little by little. Claudia screamed with delight and Floyd's dick got hard once again.

Quickly, she came off his face and demanded that he got on top of her. He complied. Her wet spot was so silky wet. He had a little trouble finding her silkiness but accidentally entered her asshole. Claudia informed him, "That's the wrong one!" Since he was not experienced, he had no idea what she was talking about. He continued. She relaxed and took it. He fucked slowly and savored every moment. He did not want to cum quickly like he did earlier. He wanted to enjoy this as long as he could. Unaware of where his dick really was, he was in heaven and Claudia was also enjoying this backdoor lovemaking.

After a long time of action, Floyd came inside her. He had no idea that he should pull out. It is not until he actually did pull out that Claudia told him, "You know you just fucked me in my ass, don't you?" Floyd was stunned. He had no idea that he actually was inside her asshole. It was so wet and juicy that it slipped right into her ass. He apologized to her, but was thrilled with how good the sex felt. He was hooked! His first sexual experience was anal and therefore, that remains his preference. After he explained this to me, it is understandable. He tells me that he enjoys pussy very much, but that the ass is truly his preferred fun.

I appreciate how Floyd has opened up to me in such a short period of time. He is really a likeable guy and I hope that we will stay in touch. It would be nice if could visit me. Money doesn't seem to be an issue. He is well-traveled, has the money to travel, and has been to a few US cities already.

After breakfast, he has a surprise for me. He tells me that he got us tickets to Germany. With the speed trains in Europe, it is only a few hours away. I am very excited and impressed with his surprise. We arrive at the station and travel to Heidelberg. It is a beautiful city. German sounds similar to Dutch – both are very guttural languages. They are not pretty at all. Heidelberg is beautiful. It is clean, safe and very scenic. There are rivers, mountains and lots of great ethnic restaurants. Heidelberg is a college town. There are a lot of American students attending university there. Despite all of the younger people living in this beautiful town, it is very quiet. Most people travel via bicycles on the old, cobblestoned streets.

We make our way to the Marktplatz (Market Place). This is a huge market with clothes, crafts, and food from all around Germany and other European countries. It is a dream-come-true for someone like myself. I buy unique German Christmas ornaments, dolls, lace place settings and hand-drawn artwork of various historical sites throughout the country. All of the shopping makes me hungry and Floyd recommends that I try some bratwurst. I soon discover that 'bratz' are delicious, one-of-a-kind sausages that are simply out of this world. Even the mustard here is amazing! Bratwurst is sold in America, but I never actually tried them before coming to

Germany. When I return home, I will be sure to buy some. No more 'regular' sausage for me.

After the Marktplatz, we go to Altstadt (Old Town). We walked around town and studied the old architecture and I bought more souvenirs. It looks like an old European village. After Altstadt, we go to the Schloss (castle) Heidelberg. There are many castles in Germany and this one, like the others, doesn't disappoint. It's massive. We take a tour in and around the castle. Instead of taking the tram up to the castle, we walk. There is a breathtaking view of the Rhine River. The gardens are beautifully maintained and look like a tranquil refuge to spend quiet time alone. We learn that this massive dwelling was built centuries ago as a wedding gift for a princess.

As we begin the final leg of our tour, we reach the apothecary, which was a pharmacy. Doctors used natural remedies for everyday aches, pains and illnesses. The apothecaries from years ago were the people's modern day drug stores. The tour was very interesting and informative.

After our exhausting day, Floyd treats me to dinner at the Indian restaurant, Taj Mahal Tandoori, which is located near the river. I shared with him before that Indian food is my favorite ethnic food. As we enter the restaurant, it is so incredibly ornate with Indian decorations that I imagine that we are in India instead of Germany. I wonder to myself just how good could this food really be? I soon discover that the food is unbelievable! I am an avid fan of Indian cuisine and the food at this restaurant, as well as the ambiance, is by far the best I have ever experienced – at home and abroad. Floyd knows how to treat a lady on a date. This has to be the best date that I have ever been on.

After dinner, we travel back to Amsterdam via the train. We are tired and we sleep on the ride back. I gently lay my head on this shoulder while he lays his head back on the headrest. We are knocked out all the way back to the station near my hotel. After such a great time, we both decide that we don't want to end the day just get. Floyd will spend the night with me in my hotel. Each of us showers first. We then watch TV and talk more about what we like to do, our hobbies, etc. We enjoy each other's company, but we are too tired to do anything sexually. With the TV on, to our surprise, we both fall fast asleep with Floyd spooning me tightly. This feels nice.

As my stay in Holland comes to an end, I try not to have any regrets. Again, I have met another great friend who has helped me discover even more about my sexuality and personality that I did not know even existed.

After we get up the next morning, we have breakfast and talk about possibly seeing each other in the future. Floyd makes it clear that he would like to visit me. I just have to let him know when. I like the idea of hosting him when he visits me in Louisiana. After we have breakfast and chat, Floyd escorts me to the lobby. Before I catch my shuttle bus to the airport, he hugs and kisses me softly and whispers in my ear, "I can't wait to come and visit you. Call me, email me - whatever. I don't want to lose touch with you. I had a great time with you, Mia. I trust you and like you a lot. Have a safe trip, baby." I am warmed by his goodbye and I am all giggles like a young teenage girl. I thank him for a wonderful time and ask a tourist to take a photo of us together. He takes one for his phone also. I want to remember him. Floyd is special. He has been a wonderful host. He is truly a charming, sweet gentleman. I am so glad that we met. Yes, the sex was totally unique and very memorable. But again, he is a great guy. Auf Wiedersehen, Floyd. I am now off to Madrid!

## "Madrid"

## 27 July, 2013

In the afternoon, I arrive in Madrid. I am fluent in Spanish and I feel much more comfortable here than I did in Holland. I quickly revert to my Castillian Spanish accent where c's and z's are pronounced as if the speaker has a lisp. Spain is the only Spanish speaking country that utilizes this type of accent or pronunciation.

Madrid is a beautiful, old, historic city. It is a very culturally rich place with the majority of the country, like most of Europe, is Catholic. I enjoy walking through the plazas and studying the artwork on the cathedrals on my way to my hotel. I am located right in the center of Madrid. I plan to take a group tour tomorrow. In the other cities, I accidentally met people who kindly showed me around. This time, I'd like to do a group tour and learn more about the history.

I had promised one of my friends that I would look up her family while staying in Spain. Honestly, I really did not want to but when you come right to a particular city, you kind of feel pressured to at least call. I find their number and I call them. They are thrilled that I contacted them. They tell me that they have some things for my friend that they want me to bring back. I hope that it is not a lot of stuff, but I kindly oblige and agree to bring the things back. I offer to come by and get them but they insist that I come for dinner. They arrange for me to come by the following night. That is fine with me. I don't have anything planned and I am just hanging out and doing whatever activity interests me. Her family lives right outside of Madrid, in a quiet rural town. When I arrive, I meet her friends, parents, and her brother. They are all very warm and welcoming. Her mom makes some unbelievable paella. I love paella. I make it now and again, but Clara's mom makes it with lots of seafood, which I love. We have delicious wine and then some rice pudding, which is a popular dessert in Spain. I am so glad that I visited and spent some time with them. They ask me countless questions about Clara. They want to know why she is not yet married and if she is dating someone. I just tell them that she dates but is very busy with work and her travels. She does not have a lot of time for socializing. They are a little worried because their son Fernando, too, is single. They want him to meet someone but he apparently enjoys being single. Fernando is a very good-looking guy. He's blond, medium height, with ice blue eyes. He does not look like his parents and sister, who are all brown-haired with brown eyes. He definitely stands out. And he is certainly a charmer. He speaks several languages and travels all around Europe as a pharmaceutical salesman. He makes good money and probably has women in different cities throughout Europe chasing after him. I guess most people would not blame him for not getting married. He is still in his 30's.

After a great meal, I decide to leave. Fernando insists on taking me back to my hotel. I concede. His parents give me a bag of goodies for Clara and I bid them farewell. I am glad that I was able to see them early on in my trip and get that 'out of the way'. But again, I am glad that I went.

On the ride back to the hotel, Fernando is quite the gentleman. We talk about a variety of different things. He wants to know how long I am staying and he wants to take me out for lunch. I tell him, "That sounds like a great idea. I'd like that". He drops me off. I thank him and go on my way. I am eager to get to my room; the bathtub is calling my name. I have some sweet smelling, soothing bubble bath. I light a candle and escape in this tub of warm water. I am very tired and lean back to enjoy my quiet time. I have enjoyed my stay so far in Europe but I am glad that it is coming to an end. It has been an unexpected whirlwind. I doze off for a bit and I think about Ken and Floyd. I think about how different they are. Even Jack was a nicer guy than Kenny. I realize that I barely know Floyd and Jack but what I do know is that they seem to be more compassionate and less self-absorbed than Kenny. Meeting other people and seeing how friendships and sex can be, I continually re-evaluate my feelings for Ken. I know I made the right choice, but it is comforting to constantly get reassured that I did. Had I stayed in New Orleans and not met such interesting people, I am pretty certain that I would be back with my ex and for what? He was an awful lover, dishonest, and narcissistic. Who needs that disappointment?

I dry myself off, rub down with some oil and climb into bed. The bed feels so warm and cozy. I need a deep, restful sleep. But first, I check my Facebook page and my email messages. I find messages from Juliette and Jack! I am pleasantly surprised. I open Juliette's first. She tells me that she misses spending time with me and she hopes that I am enjoying my trip. She also shares that she misses my kisses and that she hopes that we can rendezvous in the near future. I am hopeful that we will indeed see each other again. I write a reply to her telling her about my travels (sans the rendezvous with Floyd) and tell her that I miss her too and think about her as well. I then open Jack's email. He is still in Paris, but he will be leaving tomorrow. He tells me that he there is on business. I was thinking he was there to see a woman. Maybe he does have one there but just did not want to tell me. Nonetheless, I am glad to hear from him. I want to keep in touch with both of them. They are fun, well-cultured people with whom I have a lot of things in common. Little do they know how much they helped me get through a rough time and discover my inner sex kitten. I have found what I need and want in a relationship – sexual or platonic.

Today I go on an excursion with the other tourists from the hotel. We go to the Prado Museum, the Royal Palace, and Retiro Park. I go rowing in the lake with a few tourists. We have a ball. The park is big and very beautiful. We get back around 4:00 in the afternoon and Fernando is waiting to take me out to eat. Once our bus arrives, he is in the lobby. I feel somewhat uncomfortable about going out on a date with my friend's brother, especially since I know his parents are ready for him to meet a 'nice, single girl'. I wonder if they know he and I are meeting for dinner. Probably not. They would be all in our business. Fernando seems rather private. I will tell Clara when I get back home that her brother and I went out though.

Dinner is very good. We have empanadas – one of my favorites. We learn a lot about each other. He asks me about my situation and I tell him that I am single. He has no idea that I am in my mid-40's and I don't volunteer the information. He thinks that I am in my early 30's and I just let him think that. I need all the compliments that I can get. People really think there is something wrong with me because I have never married or had kids at my age. It is just easier to pretend I am younger. People then give me more breathing room.

Fernando and I go to a café after dinner for some dessert. We get a few unbelievable pastries and we try all of them with some strong coffee. 'Díos Mío! This is heaven!' Eating food can be so much fun and so intimate. I am going to miss the food here so much. New Orleans has good food too, but the dishes here in Europe are truly delectable.

While Fernando and I are chatting, I count my euros. I am mindful of my spending now. I really don't want to return with any foreign currency. It's harder to change back to dollars from euros. We lose money with the exchange rate. While I have my money out, I accidentally leave one of my room keys. I took two just to be on the safe side, although I figured I would really only need one key. When I realize that I left it, I forget about it. If anyone finds it, they would have no idea what the hotel and room number is.

It's late now and I ask Fernando to take me back to my hotel. He is sorry to see me leave but he understands and we head back.

We have a drink in the lobby. We exchange all of our contact information. I am surprised that he really seems to want to keep in touch with me. I am sure he will come to visit his sister eventually and we all can hang out. He is definitely very handsome and I am sure he probably has plans tonight to go out with some special lady somewhere. I bid 'Adios' to Fernando and thank him for his hospitality.

When I get to my room, I am beat. I take a shower, check my email messages, and pack up my things. I am ready to head back home. I have been away long enough. After a few hours, I climb into bed and fall asleep pretty fast. I must have been in a deep sleep. I find myself dreaming about Fernando. I have no idea why. I think back to our day today and everything that we did. The dream then takes a strange turn: I begin to dream about him in a sexy way. I did not feel that way earlier but for some reason, I do know. "Thank goodness this is a dream", I say to myself. I wouldn't want anything to happen with Clara's brother. She is a dear friend. I fall into a deeper sleep and then I have the feeling that someone has entered the room. I am knocked out lying on my stomach when all of a sudden I feel the sheets being pulled off of me. I think I must be dreaming. I then feel this warm man's body on top of me, and warm lips kissing me on my back. I begin to think that it is Fernando! But it can't be! I did not hear him open the door, undress or anything. Even though I am exhausted, I am so excited that he has come to visit me, even though this has to be a dream. He whispers in my ear with that sexy Castillian accent, "No podía dormir sabiendo que tú quedas aquí tan cerca, sola en la cama. Tuve que visitarte." (I could not sleep knowing that you are here nearby, alone in bed. I had to visit you). He turns me over and we kiss for the longest time. He turns me back over onto my stomach. He sweetly continues to kiss my back all over. It feels amazing. He reaches my ass. He kisses and gently bites my butt cheeks so attentively. He then spreads my cheeks just a bit and begins to lick my ass and pussy. I moan as I feel his warm tongue work both my holes. He gently puts his finger in and out of both my silky, wet openings. I cannot get enough of this tongue licking and eating me so good. I am moving back and forth on his tongue. Fernando is moaning as he enjoys his late night snack. He massages my butt cheeks with his hands while he licks and eats me. I play with my clit while he works my asshole. My fingers are now slipping off my clit because I am so wet. I keep rubbing my clit harder and harder like I did a few months ago by myself. I want to cum. My body needs to cum. I want more and more. I rub my clit even harder. I feel my orgasm cumming. I start to yell, "Vengo, Fernando! Sigue comiéndome, así, baby. (I'm cumming, baby. Keep eating me like that!) He works his tongue faster and he gets very excited. He feels my body start to shudder a bit. I cum really hard, screaming his name and telling him how good it feels. It's mind-blowing. I anxiously await for what comes next: He rams his rock hard, sexy dick into my pussy with such for force while he lays on my back. I am barely over my orgasm when I feel his surprisingly large dick invade my pussy. It feels so fucking good! We both whisper to each other at the same time, "Se siente tan bien." (It feels so good). This encounter is very quiet, deliberate yet powerful. Fernando reveals to me that he is about to cum. He mumbles, "Estoy veniendo ahora." I hear him let out a grunt. I know that he's just finished. I am exhausted now from this encounter. I have actually had an orgasm. I fall back into a deep sleep. When I wake in the morning, I remember my vivid dream. It was so real. The sheets are even wet. I wonder if they are wet from me playing with myself while I slept or if Fernando really visited me with that key I accidentally left on that café table. I will never know. I don't dare ask him – ever.

## "New Orleans"

## 1 August, 2013

I am finally back at home. After an unbelievable experience, it is now time to face the music with Kenny. We have to decide what to do with the house. With the way I feel, I just want to leave the house and get an apartment. We can sell it and go our separate ways. I decide to call Ken. I somehow get the courage and just call him. Surprisingly, he answers the phone right away. He is not sure whether or not I'm home. I tell him that I am back and that I need to talk to him. He is elated. He assumes that I want him back. I don't. Instead of him choosing the restaurant where we will eat, I do. I give him the time and the place. We go to Pappadeux. I get there first. I see him arrive. As he enters the restaurant, he doesn't see me at first. I wave for him to come in my direction. There is no emotion on my face. I can tell that he is put off by my coldness. He is not used to it. I was always so jolly, warm, and happy to see him. Not now. I am different. I am not the same woman he knew a month ago. I feel empowered. Confident. Enlightened. I greet saying, "Hello, Ken. How are you?" He replies, "Hi, Mia. How are you, baby? You look great. You look relaxed, but what is bothering you?" I tell him, "Nothing is bothering me. I just want to move on with my life. I really want us to sell the house and go our separate ways." He is stunned. He just assumes we would get back together. He reluctantly agrees to sell the house. After we clear that up, we order food. I relax a little bit. I needed to get that off my chest and feel in control of the situation.

Ken asks me about my trip. He says, "So what did you do? Who did you stay with? What made you go? I had no idea that you even wanted to go to Europe." I simply reply, "There is a lot of things that I want to do, Ken, but you never asked. You were never interested….I stayed with some friends. I went sightseeing and had a blast. I went to Paris, Amsterdam, Germany, and Madrid. I hope to return as soon as I can." He is impressed and says that he wishes that he went with me. I told him that it was best that I went alone. I needed the time to myself and that it was too soon after our breakup to go on such a trip together. It would have been a disaster if he went. It was better that I went without him even knowing.

I ask him, "So what did you do while I was gone? Who was the chick you were eating out in San Francisco? Why does she get all of the fun and I don't?" He clearly does not feel comfortable with the inquisition. He first apologizes for the 'incident'. There is nothing he could possibly say to make that any better. I ask him, "How would you feel if you caught me sucking some guy's dick? Wouldn't that be fucked up? You would go ballistic if you saw me doing that!" He says, "You're right, Mia. I wasn't thinking about it in those terms. I was just being stupid and selfish. I am so sorry for everything. It was not worth us breaking up." I ask him, "Who in the hell is she anyway?" He says, "She is a client of mine. We've messed around off and on for the past few months. She doesn't mean anything to me. My sales have skyrocketed with me messing with her. I did it to increase my sales revenue. The more revenue I bring in, the bigger my bonus at the end of the year. As crazy as it seems, I did it for the money, Mia. I know I am an asshole but she has helped me to become one of the top salesmen." At this point, nothing really surprises me anymore. He just proves to me again and again, that I am better off without him. I don't want to be with someone who doesn't respect me enough not to fuck someone else, let alone tear their pussy up. I am so over this dude. I finish my meal. I tell him, "I will contact our real estate agent and have her start the ball rolling right away. I will move out within the month, so you can move back in if you want. I will get an apartment somewhere. I just can't do this anymore. Thanks for dinner." I leave and feel totally disgusted. This man sucks the life and energy out of me. I need to get as far away from him as possible. I leave and head out to my car. Without my knowing it, Ken follows me out to my car. He won't let it go. He asks to talk to me inside my car. I am not crazy about the idea but I agree – like an idiot. He continues this pointless conversation in my car about how we can work things out and that he still loves me. I couldn't care less. I know that it is over, but I feel like we should say goodbye one last time. Out of the blue, he kisses me. Half-heartedly, I reciprocate. We start whispering shit to each other, trying to get the other turned on. I say to him, "Are you gonna miss this pussy, baby? You didn't really want this. Did you?" He gets upset but still gets aroused. He has something to prove to me. Ken pulls off of my panties and explores my wet pussy. He quickly puts his fingers in his mouth and sucks them. He smiles and says, "Damn, that tastes good!" He pulls his dick like he was doing a magic trick. It is rock hard, standing straight up. I must admit: I'm turned on. I tell him, "What do you expect me to do now?" We kiss and I stroke the hell out of his dick. We both are getting so hot and turned on. He reaches over and puts my seat all the way back, so that it lies flat. I lay down. He gets on top of me, but not all the way. He positions himself so that he can put his dick in my mouth. He moves his hips back and forth in my mouth like it is my pussy. I suck it so good for him. My mouth is so warm and wet. His eyes are closed as he enjoys his slow, wet, juicy blowjob. I moan as I pleasure him. I am enjoying this too. All the while, I know this will be the last time we are intimate. I want to leave him with a lasting impression. He sounds like he is about to cum. I tell him, "Fuck my pussy, Ken!" He is turned by my order. Without hesitation and about to explode, he forcefully plunges his dick into me. Like most times, it does not last very long. I know he enjoyed the blowjob and the pussy. It wasn't great for me but now I can say goodbye to this idiot for good. Hasta la vista, Ken!

# "Thanksgiving"

## New Orleans, LA

## 28 November, 2013

The holiday season is here. I enjoy spending time with family and friends. I have dinner with my parents and see all of my relatives. It is not terribly comfortable. Everyone is asking where Ken is. I have to explain to them that we have broken up and even though they don't know the details, they think that it is my fault. They saw him as a good catch with a good job. If they only knew!!

After dinner, I meet with a few girlfriends and we go out for drinks. I am well overdue. I have not seen my friends in ages. We catch up on everything. I don't share with them what happened in Europe. It's a little embarrassing. I did not intend for all of that to happen but it did. Friends, especially female friends, tend to get jealous sometimes, or hold things against us at some point. I don't feel like being judged or have what I told them be thrown back into my face months down the road.

With that said, my friends to tell me that they want to go to a New Year's Eve party. I think it is a great idea. I am down with the idea. I really don't want to stay home and watch the ball drop all alone eating popcorn this year. People say that whatever you are doing at that time is what you will do for the rest of year. If you are out partying, you will party a lot that year. If you are having sex, you will get laid regularly that year. And if you are being bored and not having a celebration, you will have a quiet, boring year. I don't know if this is true or not, but what the hell? Why find out if it is true? I'd rather be having fun!

They tell me about a swinger party at a local hotel. My one friend, Anne Marie, has close friends who swing. Off and on, she would share stories with us about her friends' adventures and her boyfriend. They have been in the lifestyle for quite a while. For them, it makes their relationship exciting and spontaneous. We were always so riveted by the stories. They sounded like something you would see on Real Sex on HBO or something from an erotic novel. I have always been curious but too scared to actually go to a swinger party. But once Anne Marie tells us about the New Year's Eve fête, all of us are on board and very much looking forward to that evening.

Even though I had a great time in Europe, I was by myself and my encounters were private and special to me. I don't necessarily feel comfortable behaving the same way with my friends. Despite the fact that I look forward to this party, as far as my friends are concerned, I am still fairly reserved and rather traditional.

This New Year's Eve party is extremely confidential. We have to register and pay up front to attend. They want our names, ages and addresses, but they keep everything very much on the down low. The four of us pay our money and provide all of the required information. About a week later, we get a list of attendees (with number ID's instead of names), their professions, and the cities they will be coming from. They are all professional people. There will be required attire: facial masks. Elements of this party remind me of the 'Eyes Wide Shut' movie. This will allow everyone to have fun and be totally anonymous. It sounds sexy.

As time progresses, I get more and more excited. I am not sure what to wear. Some people will wear lingerie and others will dress in sexy outfits. This will be my first swinger party, so I need to know the do's and don'ts.

By this time, I now have my new apartment. I live about 45 minutes away from the old house. I like not being so close to him. My apartment is small and quaint. It's clean and I have great neighbors. It is totally opposite to what I was used to. Before, I had an elaborate home. Now, I am very content with plain and simple surroundings. All of the glitz and glamour are no longer important to me.

I have a mini house warming. All of my girlfriends bring me some household gifts and linens to get me started off. We have a fun girls' night with great wine, delicious appetizers and tasty desserts. We then start to talk about our New Year's Eve outing. All of us are excited and very much looking forward to it. Unexpectedly, we are all single this year; two are divorced, I just broke up with my boyfriend, and the other has been single for a while. We all decide to wear sexy outfits to the party since this is our first time – no lingerie. None of us feel comfortable wearing anything skimpy there. We also talk about how we don't have to do anything, if we don't want to. We decide to stay together but at least in two's, if we get separated. One Saturday, we go to the mall and do our sexy clothes shopping. We find a boutique with sexy, tight clothes. Generally, we all dress rather conservatively but New Year's Eve night will not be a night to dress like a librarian, so-to-speak. I pick out a short black skirt with a pretty chartreuse colored, button down blouse. I will make sure that many of the buttons will be undone that night. My friends buy short dresses in bright, sexy colors – fuchsia, turquoise, and lavender. Their dresses are form fitting and low cut. The belts accentuate their small waists. They will wear fishnet or sheer stockings with their 4" to 5" shoes. I plan to wear sheer black, thigh high stockings with 5" sexy black suede boots. Later, we find a shop and buy our masks. The masks are so colorful and decorative. They match our outfits perfectly.

Finally, we head to Victoria's Secret. We all find bra and panty sets that match our individual outfits, since our undergarments will be seen that night. With these fierce, sexy outfits we will surely recognize each other easily.

We discover that at the event, no cell phones are allowed. We have to leave them behind. I guess they are fearful that people may take videos or pictures of people in compromising positions. Once again, there will be all types of people there – doctors, lawyers, educators, journalists, CEO's, etc. We all decide to buy some condoms too, just in case. I really don't want to do anything but I would rather be safe than sorry. I like to watch and that is what I plan to do that night mostly – watch, watch, and watch!

# "Work Christmas Party"

## 13 December, 2013

The holiday parties and happy hours have been a lot of fun. It is freeing to come and go as I please. I like being alone. If I want to go somewhere, I go. If I don't, I just stay home.

Last year, I had so many events to attend with Ken, our friends, and family. This year is so quiet. The holiday party at work is just what I need to lift my spirits. All of the employees, the partners, and their spouses will be there. It is always a hoot to see people get drunk and make total, complete asses of themselves. For me, that is the best part!

One of my colleagues, Lorenzo, is a gem. He is very helpful and is always looking out for me. He knows somehow that I have been struggling with some things lately and he is a really comforting and helpful person to have in the office. I always ask him for advice when I am not sure about something and we have lunch together sometimes. I have noticed that he is quite handsome, and just my type. He is tall, well-built, and charming.

At the holiday party, he sits next to me and we eat and have some drinks. We have a really lovely time. Luckily, our party is at a hotel, so we can stay in case one of us cannot drive home. That is reassuring. I tend to drink too much at times when I am with close friends, but I rarely drink in public. Even though I don't generally get wasted, this year has been so bad, that I may overdue it.

Anyway, Lorenzo and I continue hanging out. He is funny and we have a good time together. The music is pretty good. We dance and have a good time. The party is in full swing. We exchange compliments and warm smiles. The music and the alcohol are making for a very interesting evening for sure. He asks me, "Do you want to leave, Mia?" I say, "Sure. What do you have in mind?" He says, "Why don't we go out on the town for a bit and then we can come back here." I say, "Okay. Sounds good. Lead the way." He smiles and we leave to catch a cab. He politely puts his hand on my knee. It's not inappropriate. It's comforting. I know that he likes me and I feel the same way. I have no idea where we are going. He is in charge, which is kind of sexy. I like a man to be in charge as long as he is disciplined, respectful, and has it together financially. We get to our first stop. It's a classy restaurant and bar. The music is old school R & B. Although it's packed with people, we are able to find a secluded small table where we can talk. We are sitting pretty close together; our knees are touching under the table. As I hear everyone talking in the distance, I am looking and listening to Lorenzo talk. Meanwhile, my mind is off somewhere else in a place of unbelievable kisses, lovemaking, and orgasms. I am getting soaking wet and I feel waves of excitement pass through my body off and on as I think of what I hope we may eventually do. I try to stay focused on what he is saying but it is almost impossible. I am checking his body out without trying to be obvious. It is a treat for me to be near someone who I am so attracted to. Lorenzo's arms and shoulders look amazing. I stare at his face. He has such dazzling eyes and a sexy smile. I gaze at his lips intently. That really catches his attention. He startles me and asks, "Mia, what are you looking at, my dear?" I come out of my daze and say, "I was admiring your smile. That's all".

He smiles again and leans towards me and says in a seductive whisper, "Oh, you were just looking at my smile? I bet you want these lips to kiss you long and softly, don't you?" I shut my eyes for moment and have to gain my composure. I am ready for him to grab me and kiss me. I open my eyes back up and reply, "Actually, yes. That would be nice. You look like a good kisser." Lorenzo then plants a sweet, slow kiss on my lips. His lips are warm and soft, just as I imagined. He is such a gentleman. We are now sitting very close to each other. Lorenzo comments on my perfume and tells me that it is turning him on. The attraction keeps building between us. I look down at his crotch and see that he is hard. He catches me looking at his dick and says, "See what you did?" We both have painted grins on our faces and decide it's time to go. He calls for the check, pays for it and we leave. We go to another place for drinks. This other bar has a cozy, intimate ambiance inside. It's the perfect place for us. We gently continue to kiss each other throughout the evening. Eventually, Lorenzo says, "Do you want to go back to the hotel now? I want to show you how much

I like you, Mia." I agree and say, "Sure. Let's go. It'll be better for us to be all alone."

When we finally get to the hotel, we kiss like crazy in the elevator. I am soaking wet now and he is so hard! Once we approach the room, he can't get the key out fast enough! He struggles to get the door open, but he eventually does. As soon as we are inside, we rip off each other's clothes, kissing like lunatics. We barely make it onto the bed. We can't get there fast enough. I tell him, "Turn on the light. I want to see everything!" He pulls off my dress, sucks the hell out of my tits and pulls down my panties. Lorenzo spreads my legs wide and starts sucking on my clit and licking my pussy. As soon as he starts to eat me, he mumbles, "Mia, your pussy tastes so good. I can't believe your pussy is in my face! It's so wet and juicy. You drive me crazy! I have dreamed about this moment so many times in my head." My back arches while my legs are draped over his back. I gently grab his head and hold it steady between my legs, moaning and groaning the whole time. I look down and see him generously letting spit drip onto my pussy making it unbelievably wet! I get turned on watching Lorenzo's spit dripping from his mouth onto my pussy like that. I beg him to fuck me but he refuses. He wants to make me cum with his tongue first. He cups my ass with his hands and licks my clit and pussy with circular, slurping strokes and I cum so hard. I scream out his name and pull him up to kiss him. I can't wait to taste my juices on his sexy lips and tongue. It drives me insane. No longer after, he plunges his dick into my super wet throbbing pussy so fast and hard. The feeling was like nothing either of us had ever felt. It was a feeling of total ecstasy. We both let out the loudest gasps of incredible pleasure when he first rammed his dick into my pussy. With each thrust, we moaned, kissed, held each other tight and yelled together. Our bodies are connected and totally in sync. I feel an orgasm on the horizon. I tell him, "I'm about to cum." I start talking the crazy shit, "Oh my God!! Shit, baby! I'm cumming!!" I cum first and then he cums right after me. He yells so loudly. He tells me my pussy is so good and that he fantasized about being with me every time he watched me walk by him in the office.

After our session, we take a shower together. We dry each other off. Lorenzo has a masculine, sweet, clean smell, which turns me on. I am putting lotion on standing in front of the bedroom mirror, which is a few feet away from the bed. I can see Lorenzo watch me as I do my evening routine. He observes my curves, realizing that he is slowly getting acquainted with my whole body. This gives him a sense of pleasure and also disbelief.

I brush my hair and put on my flimsy, see- through bra and panty set. I am plain - not wearing any makeup with wet hair pulled back. I am totally natural. Lorenzo likes to see me like that at night. He tells me that I look natural and sexy. I get into bed with him while he stares. The bed is warm and I am glad to be next to him under the covers. He offers to give me a massage. I jump at the offer. I lay on my stomach as he unbuttons my bra. I am so excited to get a massage from him. Lorenzo is a phenomenal masseur. I feel his sexy body straddle my butt. I then feel his two strong oiled hands firmly grab my shoulders. He kneads my shoulders and arms so well. He moves over onto my back rubbing and slowly kneading it. I am in heaven feeling his warm, strong hands invade my back. He forcefully massages his hands into my skin. My body gently gets pushed down into the bed and pillows with the perfect force. I let out sighs of delight each time he delivers a touch to my skin.

He moves down to my legs. He works with each one. He starts with my thigh, calf and then down to my feet. He works on my feet for a while. I am in ecstasy. He grabs each one with both hands and rubs them with the warm oil. He gives particular attention to the bottom of my feet. I am thrilled with this message. All the while, my pussy is getting wetter and wetter. I don't say anything. It is late and I think he may want to go to sleep. He turns me over and gets more oil. His strong hands grab my big breasts. He squeezes and rubs them so perfectly. My nipples get harder with each grip. I moan and tell him how good it feels.

Intermittently, I feel his dick press against me. It makes me impatient. I don't feel like waiting anymore. I tell him, "It's time for round two. Put your dick in my pussy, baby". He listens to my demand and gently puts it in.

This goes on for weeks. We're like kids in a candy store. We both enjoy having his dick inside my pussy, but every time he enters me, it's just as thrilling as the time before – maybe more. He looks into my eyes, kissing me and making me wetter and wetter. I start to talk shit in his ear and I feel his dick get even harder. I can tell he is about to cum. Lorenzo moans and lets out a grunt, which I love to hear and he climaxes really hard.

I am so relaxed that my body feels like jelly. I roll onto my stomach. I start to go to sleep. All of a sudden, I feel Lorenzo's tongue licking my butt cheeks and my asshole. I am so surprised but it feels so unreal. He licks my pussy and ass up and down in a sexy rhythmic motion that drives me insane. His incredible tongue goes up and down and swirls all around. He grabs my ass in his hands and gently squeezes my cheeks while he licks my asshole and pussy. I take my finger and start to play with my clit. In no time, I feel myself start to cum. I start screaming and he gets excited too. My pussy juices flow slowly onto his tongue as I cum from his incredible licking. After I cum, he is ready to go again. He rams his dick into my pussy while I am still on my stomach. He tells me it's so tight since I just came and that he can hardly get it in. He tries and tries and eventually, it goes in slowly. His face is in my hair while he pumps me harder and harder. He's breathing so hard. He grabs my breasts and he cums so hard on my ass. We both feel so complete and content. Now we are both truly exhausted. He holds me tight as we both fall fast asleep.

# "New Orleans"

## 26 December, 2013

Lorenzo and I have been having a blast. He is such a fun person. We have a wonderful time together. We have lots is common. He is doting, romantic, can cook, and has a smile to die for. I cannot believe that I am so lucky. He is younger than I am. It bothers me that if we continue to date, he may want kids. I am 46; it's not impossible, I guess. He seems to be content with not having kids at the moment.

He and I go out quite a bit. That is one of the luxuries of not having kids – we just pick up and go when we want. One night we go to a Thai restaurant. The lighting is perfect. We get a small table, sitting close to each other. He likes the way I am dressed. I have on a pretty black dress with high heels. During the entire dinner, we exchange a lot of eye contact, which gets us both really excited. He focuses on my lips, admiring them, and probably imagining his fat dick in my mouth. I am staring at him and fantasizing about licking the outline of his lips with my tongue slowly. I stare at his sexy, mesmerizing eyes and get turned on every time he smiles or just looks at me.

We leave the restaurant and make our way to a bar playing some really good music. We start to have some drinks. We get more and more relaxed. We are sitting close to each other. Lorenzo has his hand up my dress and he massages the inside of my thighs under the table. I can feel myself getting aroused. He doesn't know that I am not wearing any panties and I can feel my juices streaming.

We decide it's time to leave and get back to his place. The whole drive back, we kiss every chance we get. He finally takes his fingers and explores my pussy. His fingers slip and slide. He places his finger inside me and we both let out a loud moan. He asks me, "Why didn't you tell me you weren't wearing any panties?" I reply, "I wanted to surprise you." He pulls his finger back out and sucks on it and then I put it in my mouth and have my turn.

We finally get back to Lorenzo's place. We are kissing each other so passionately. We are smiling and having a great time, like always. He is holding me tight, walking to the bed. He lays me down and pulls my dress up and starts to eat my pussy so good. He loves how wet it is. He sticks his finger in and out while sucking on my clit. My pussy is so tight and wet that every time he sticks his finger in, it gets sucked right in. I start to cum and go crazy. After I cum, I get up, take off his shirt and turn him over onto his back. I then begin to gently kiss his neck and chest. I love the way his big, strong body feels against mine. His cologne turns me on even more. I work my way down to his stomach and then to his beautiful, chocolate stick. I enjoy feeling him in my mouth and hearing him moan and groan and grab my hair. I don't want him to come yet.

We continue to kiss and look into each other's eyes and smile. He gently puts his manhood inside of me but it's not my pussy. I tell him, "That's the wrong one. But wait. It's okay." He asks me, "Are you sure?" I say, "Yes". It was so wet and I was so relaxed from the wine and he was so gentle, that it felt so good. He keeps saying how tight it is and how good it feels. He slowly keeps going and tells me he is about to cum. He then pulls it out and cums all over my stomach. We both shower, turn on some music and I lie on his chest and relax. What a wonderful lover I have!

### "New Year's Eve Party Time"

### New Orleans, LA

### 31 December, 2013

My friends and I are so excited that New Year's Eve is finally here. We've been planning for this night since November. We bought new clothes, did our research, and have dreamed about what we might do at the party. Even though I am really excited, I am pretty nervous because I have no idea what to expect. I imagine going to swinger parties can be awkward. What if someone is attracted to me but I am not to them? I do not like hurting people's feelings. From my understanding, most in attendance will be couples. There will be food, dancing, and good music. There will rooms where people will actually be doing it, and there are glass windows for the voyeurs, like myself. Other rooms don't have any windows. Those people prefer to be more private. My friends and I have rehearsed what we should and shouldn't do tonight. We will stick together but, if worse comes to worse, we break up into duos.

We plan to leave around 7:30. Everyone will meet here at my place since I live closest to the venue. We will have drinks and some tapas before we leave. We want to feel satisfied and not go there feeling starved.

I really wanted to spend New Year's with Lorenzo, but since I already made plans with my girls, they would not let me back out. He understood. We will get together tomorrow. He will bring in the New Year with some of his friends too. It's good for couples to have some breathing room. It's probably not good to be together all the time. But it's fun though. If I had my way, I would be with Lorenzo 24/7. I don't want to scare him away though. Most men enjoy their space. I always enjoyed my space before, but not with Lorenzo. I would love to eat with him, shop with him, sleep with him every night – the whole shebang. But again, I want to tread carefully.

Finally, my friends arrive. Everyone looks so spectacular; the masks are beautiful and our outfits coordinate with the masks. Our shoes are dazzling and we are ready for an unforgettable night of once-in-a-lifetime fun. We have some strong margaritas, sangria, and some shots. We listen to some old school rap and hip-hop – Biggie, Snoop, Mary J. Blige, Tupac – all the hot artists from the early 90's. After an hour or so of partying, we are on our way. The cab comes and picks us up. I feel sorry for the driver. We are loud and cracking up the whole way. We are a little obnoxious. But what the hell? It's New Year's Eve; we'll give him a big tip.

We get to the venue. At the spot, we have to rent a locker to store our cell phones. They check our ID's against our registration information. We take off our masks so they can check our faces against our photo identifications. It is very organized. Then, they ask us to walk through a metal detector and they check our bags for weapons. I like that they are so cautious. I will feel safer and enjoy myself more. I am very impressed and look forward to having a good time. My girlfriends do not share my sentiments, but they don't let the heavy security dampen their excitement too much.

Finally, we get onto the main floor. It is very big and there are already a good hundred people there.

Everyone is wearing a mask. Some are dressed a little scantily and others, like us, have on sexy but tasteful outfits. I am sure that I know some people here, but I will not figure it out unless I get close enough to hear their voices.

The music is really good. Everyone is feeling mellow. Most drinks are included with the door price. With the alcohol flowing, people are very brave and extra friendly. It is strange that men hit on us even though they are with their women. Most instances, their wives and girlfriends are not next to them, but they too are mingling and meeting people. These couples are truly here to have fun and they trust their partners to do what feels comfortable and natural to them. I could never be like that with Lorenzo, even though our relationship is still very new. And honestly, I doubt that he could be that way with me either. In any event, this is a fun change of pace. I am anxious to see what happens and if my girlfriends hook up with someone.

My friend, Katia, meets an interesting guy. He is white and definitely her type – blond, blue eyed, tall and handsome. He looks Northern European. Through the mask, she can see his mesmerizing blue eyes. He's tall, built and has a great smile. They dance for a while and then he takes her by some of the glass windowed rooms to watch some couples have some fun. Katia likes the voyeuristic entertainment. She never thought she would be into voyeurism, but she really likes it. I have always found it to be very sexy and hot. I like how the 'performers' love being watched and purposely put on a show. They are true exhibitionists. Apparently, the couples in those rooms did not disappoint Katia and her blue-eyed friend.

My friend, Jenna, meets a married couple. They are a good-looking Latin couple. The wife is gorgeous with the signature red lipstick and curvy body. She stands about 5'8" with heels. Her husband has a medium build and is very caliente. He is dreamy with dark hair and dark eyes. They both have olive skin. Jenna has always had a thing for Latin men. She talks to them for a while and discovers that the husband and wife swing together. They do not do full swap, only soft swap (only the women in an intimate encounter sleep together.) The wife wants to sleep with my friend while the husband watches. If Jenna agrees, the experience may blossom into a threesome. They will let Jenna decide…

I have my eyes on a handsome, tall guy who seems to be checking me out. In fact, he reminds me a lot of Lorenzo - his walk, his mannerisms, his lips. I feel like I need to get closer so that I can get a better look. Eventually, I make my way over to him. He is talking with his friends and then I see him check out ladies as they walk by. Now that I am right up on this gentleman, I see that he is Lorenzo's height. He has his lips and eyes. It looks just like him. I need to hear his voice. When I finally hear his voice, I will know whether or not it is really him.

I get up my nerve to approach him. I say, "Hello. How are you?" He grins and says, "Hi. I swear that I know you from somewhere." I tell him, "I am sure you say that to all the ladies. I see you appreciate boobs and ass." He gets embarrassed and says, "Guilty as charged. That is why I have been checking you out, Mia. I thought that was you. Did you figure out this was me?" My heart sank. I really did not expect to run into Lorenzo here like this. I ask him, "Why didn't you tell me you were coming here tonight?" He then asks me, "And why didn't you mention it to me either, babe?" We both get quiet. I replied, "I didn't know how you would react and since we just started dating, I may have turned you off with this. Besides, we bought our tickets months ago." Lorenzo smiles and responds, "I was really afraid that you would think that I was a freak, so I treaded carefully with you. You seem very conservative, Mia. I really like you and I didn't want to turn you off. I really did want to tell you, but I assumed you would not react well. My friends told me to keep quiet when we bought our tickets a while back. So, I just left it alone and decided to stay mum about this event. I hope you are not angry with me. I want you to trust me, Mia. I really, really like you." I reassuringly tell Lorenzo, "I really like you too. You can tell me anything. We are adults and we have lives outside of our new relationship – friends, family, co-workers, etc. Just talk to me and I will talk to you too. We have a great relationship. We don't want to do anything that could jeopardize what we have just discovered." After our chat, we are both so relieved. We hug and kiss and get to business! We decide to use this to our advantage. He takes me by the hand. We go to a secluded room with no windows. We kiss and make out. This is so hot! He forcefully bends me over the bed and fucks the shit out of me so hard. He has never fucked me so hard before and it was so unbelievable! The evening, the ambience – everything – got us so turned on. This has been a great experience. We leave the room and find our friends. We are holding hands and very thrilled with our discovery. We are delighted to actually bring the New Year in together.

I have a feeling that 2014 will be a great year. Out with the old and in with the new. I cannot wait to see what adventures await Lorenzo and me. I think we can get used to this swinging lifestyle!

**THE END**

We hope you enjoyed this exciting book! Our only wish is that you get out there and have some Blissful Encounters of your own!

Made in the USA
Charleston, SC
22 February 2014